DAY DEATH

A BRUTES OF BRISTLEBROOK PREQUEL NOVELLA

REBECCA QUINN

Cover by Justine Bergman at JAB Design Studio.

ISBN: 978-1-923196-00-1

CONTENT NOTE

Hello lovely Quinnksters,

I'm so freaking thrilled you've come back to check out Day Death and follow our Brutes and our gal back into the past. Thank you so, so much for all your support. You truly can't know how much I appreciate it.

Before we get started, I'd like to address a few important things. Firstly, I would like to gently direct everyone to my website, rebeccaquinnauthor.com, where there is a list of all tropes and content warnings for this book.

Day Death is bleak, and sad, and deals with a wide range of scenes and situations that readers may find triggering, so I would encourage everyone to look those over before proceeding.

As with all my books, I've tried to be as comprehensive as I could with that list, but please, if you have any questions or concerns, or believe anything should be added, contact me at rebecca.quinn.author@gmail.com

Secondly, on the above note, I'd like to specifically call out the fact that this book deals heavily with bombings, looting, gun violence, grief, suicidal ideation, loss of family members and friends and much more. Your mental health matters, so please be kind to yourself and seek support if you need it.

Finally, this book also deals with a BDSM scene and dynamics. Please be mindful that this is fiction, and shouldn't be taken as instructional reading. Liberties are taken for the sake of the story, events are dramatized, and dynamics move faster in fictional, apocalyptic worlds than they do in life.

If you're inspired to try any new kink, please communicate extensively with your partner, research non-fiction, reputable sources of information, and always, always, keep things safe, sane, and consensual (or insert the appropriate kink acronym of your choice).

Okay, Becky's safety lecture is once again complete. Now go and get your heart broken!

Lots of love,

Becky Quinn

Episode One

Jaykob

Something's wrong with the air tonight. It's been messing with me since I left my stupid, freezing trailer and came to the club, and I can't work out why. It happens sometimes, like I can't draw a breath right. Or like I've held it too long and something feels about to burst.

It usually happens out on deployment, and usually when we're not only up shit creek, but drowning in it. It happens in that loaded second after a bomb hits, when the light's burning out your retinas, but before the sound finally blasts your eardrums and you're slammed with the shockwave.

The air gets tense.

Prickly.

Full of . . . *something*.

I felt it when that sniper had me squared in his sights back in the sandpit before I was dragged for cover, and that time our chopper skirted a no-fly zone and nearly got wiped for it.

The air felt like this the day Ryan died.

But I'm not on deployment, and I don't have anyone to get

my dick in a knot about anymore, so I don't know why I'm getting that feeling now.

I've been back for weeks, and there sure as hell ain't any bombs or snipers in this prissy kink club. It's a clear night, the news has got nothing useful to say—big fucking surprise—and everyone else is calm. Don't know why I'm so on edge.

It must be one of those things Jasper used to run his mouth about in our debriefings before he retired. Bringing your shit home with you or whatever. Head doctor crap. Head doctor crap and the kind of woo woo fortune-telling bullshit that gullible idiots pay nine ninety-nine a minute for.

I need to shake it off.

"One minute," Dom warns.

Beside me, Thomas edges back behind the start line, and I ignore his grin. Guy has a pretty face, the kind women giggle about, but that grin makes him look like a gofer. He might watch my six when we're on a tour, but here at Darkside? Asshole always cheats.

My eyes are on the shifting shadows of the deep gardens. Vines hang like nooses between the trees, and the thumping bass of the club behind me throbs through my veins.

None of it makes my skin any less twitchy.

"Remember, the Darkside safeword is red. Any submissive wearing a yellow band is off limits except for their dominant. For this hunt, we've got hard limits on breath and blood play. Light pain only, with consent, and the usual club rules apply. There are club monitors throughout the gardens, so use your whistles if you need assistance." Dom pauses, looking us over one by one. He glances at his watch, then cocks a brow. "Happy hunting."

The siren blares, harsh and teeth-jarring, and neon red lights sputter on overhead, igniting the garden in a flickering crimson nightmare. It's too much like the images that make me wake in the night covered in sweat, but I shove that aside. I've been waiting all week for this hunt.

Thomas is already rushing forward, leaving the start line seconds before Dom's go-ahead. I yank him from behind, and as he jerks back, off balance, I kick his ankles out from under him so he slams to the ground with an *oof*.

"Really, Jayk?" Dom says dryly, and I shrug, stepping over Thomas.

The other dominants run through the darkness, strung out on the urgency of the panicky lights, the alert that screeches the way my ma used to, like it's all a high and they've never taken a hit before.

I stalk past all of them until the trees swallow me whole.

The foliage dampens some of the siren's shriek, but the shifting bodies, the bomb-fire shadows, they turn me edgy, thuggish. Hyper-awareness pricks down my spine. My pulse pants its need to find prey.

To capture.

To trap.

The tension makes me hungry.

I keep a steady pace. The subbies were let loose ten minutes ago, and the gardens circle the whole gaudy ass club. By now, they could be anywhere. Charging around like a drunken bull ain't going to help anything. They need to be tracked—flushed out.

Fat chance of that now.

I study the ground. The trees. There are tracks everywhere,

scored and mussed by the heavy-footed idiots thundering ahead of me. Some of the doms buddy up into pairs or packs like this is some corporate trust exercise. Like if they actually manage to catch a sub—doubtful—they'll clap each other on the back, self-congratulate themselves for their *teamwork* and *share*.

I'd rather pick my eyeballs out with a toothpick.

There's a clear track leading off to my right, wide and brightly lit. To my left . . . there's only a glut of red-drenched darkness. Tiny trails cut into the gloom—shadowed enough to feel hidden but broad enough that a nervous subbie could scurry through at a decent pace.

I turn left.

There are fifteen dominants out on this hunt, and only seven submissives—two of those subbies are paired off with their doms and are off-limits for this hunt, and another one is Hugh, who ain't my type. That leaves four targets. Just four, to thirteen hunters.

Not that it matters.

They may be hunters, but they're not competition.

Most of them are playactors who find the stage once a week when Darkside's doors open. Maybe they paddle some subbie's ass or jack themselves off with their hand around someone's throat—but whatever their kink, so many of these assholes are the same. They'll pack their shit all away on Monday morning, head back to their cushy little office jobs and strangle their needs with a Hermés tie that costs more than my entire wardrobe. They'll filter themselves with all of that mannered crap—the small talk and pleasantries, the pretty clothes and the white lies —and they'll pretend that a few hours is enough to satisfy every raw craving that makes them ache at night.

Twigs crack under my boots like bones. Adrenaline makes

my skin hot and sensitive to every scrape of silken leaves. The siren sounds like a scream in the dark, and it's really fucking with my head. I *hate* screaming. It throws me back to places I don't want to go.

Those places are why I'm different, though. That, and the fact that I don't have a Hermés tie, and I don't strangle *shit*. Darkside, these hunts, they're the one place I can let loose without it being a "problem." Out here, I'm not a fuck up. Out here, my skin fits right. I can focus on what I was made to do.

And I was made to hunt. To find.

To *fuck*.

A branch snaps to my right, and I turn, twisting through the trees. My pulse thunders in my ears, eating the siren's wails. The shadows are eerie, alive. Anticipation sharpens my breaths. The stormy flickering of the crimson light sparks something feral in my blood that demands a response. It bleeds into the twitchy feeling that's been chasing me.

But nothing stirs.

The small hairs on my arms lift. At the back of my neck. The stillness is unnatural, the usual rustles disturbed. I've been enlisted too long now not to trust my instincts. Been on too many raids, and out in too many forests, and bunkers, and weapons facilities. In the last three years, I've lost count of how many times our unit has been deployed.

I know this feeling.

I'm not alone.

The chilly thrill of being watched makes my stomach give a low, hungry flip. And it's better here. Out here, I'm not thinking about the guys being safe, or if my head's about to be confetti.

Out here, the only threat is me.

I step forward again, and leaves cut battle lines across my cheeks. My breath shivers the foliage by my mouth. I look down —there are gentle smears in the dirt around my feet.

Raising my head, I breathe deep. I smell flowers, but it sure as hell ain't natural. It's pungent, too unnaturally sweet.

Slowly, I crane my head up. Wide green eyes peer down at me from between the branches.

Alice.

Satisfaction rips through me like a drone strike.

Single. Started coming a few months ago . . . and there's no protective yellow band for little Alice. No protection for her pretty eyes, or her fragile mouth, or her plush pussy.

I circle the base of the tree, lust heating me through. "Down. Now."

She pulls herself up higher on the tiny branch, but it bows under her and she freezes. Color rides high on her cheeks. The woman is soft and curvy, maybe mid-twenties, and her blonde hair has the tender glow of someone who can drop big bucks on products.

I want to smear dirt all through it.

"I ain't a climber, subbie. You won't like what I do if you make me come up there." I smirk, standing half in the shadows. The neon beams flare at my back. They turn her red—a perfect target. "Last chance."

She shakes her head fearfully, and my smirk widens. Because she knows what she is. She's lost in the woods, and I'm the big bad wolf.

And I am. Fucking. *Starved.*

I reach up, fingers brushing the branch, and Alice squeals, pulling back, but there's nowhere to go but down. Stalking closer to the bowed end of the branch, I stand on my toes and manage to wrap both hands around it.

Looking into her nervous eyes, I pull the slender branch down.

I feel the strain in my back, my biceps, but slowly, so slowly, the branch begins to dip. The closeness of her, the dizzying mess of sounds and lights and speed, it makes me hungry. It makes me *want*.

"Wait," she whispers, staring at me, down at the branch, at the ground, then back at me. "Wait, wait."

My cock thickens. At her protests. At the carnal, promising scent of her. At her quick breaths, and the color that's pooling from her cheeks down her neck and across her chest above the flimsy little white dress she's wearing.

Instead of answering, I move one hand down the branch, clasping it again closer to her as it bows even further, and red lights flicker over us. Then I shift my other hand, moving closer and closer, until the branch is dipped almost to my chest level and I'm less than a foot away from her.

Straining, I reach out and brush her skin.

That seems to startle her into motion, and she shrieks, then jumps from the tree. It's only a short drop, but I watch her closely to make sure she lands clean before I release the branch. She keeps her feet under her, but as she turns to run, she stumbles.

I'm on her kneeling form in moments, wrapping one arm round her waist and a hand around her chin and hauling her back against me. Her pulse hammers against my palm, her body squirming against me as she struggles. It's almost too easy to hold her, but it ain't as easy to hold her right—she's soft and frantic and fragile, and I could snap her by accident.

But I like the fight.

My dick is thick and hard against her grinding ass, and I bite her earlobe.

"Do you want to get fucked, subbie?" I growl.

Out of the corner of my eye, I see a shift of movement, and my head whips around. Dom looks at the both of us, then nods at me, stepping back into the shadows but staying within hearing distance. Fucker. Doesn't matter if he's on base as my captain, or here as a club monitor, the dick is always watching over my shoulder.

Realizing my subbie still hasn't responded, I loosen my grip. "Answer, Alice."

"Let me go," she moans, but she rubs her ass against me again, and I grunt.

I'm hot, oversensitive. My cock is throbbing. I want to fuck against her—but not until I get a clear *yes*. She's practically a stranger, and these games can fuck with your head. Mine is already too twisted up.

I release her chin, and tangle my hand in her hair, yanking her head back against my shoulder. I bury my nose in the strands, and sure as fuck, it smells like money—sweet and pungent and reeking of cash. My fist tightens, and when she flinches at the pressure, my cock aches, straining painfully against my zipper.

"No deal. You know the rules." With my free hand, I trace the wet inner rim of her stickily glossed lips. Alice is pretty— I'm not blind, I noticed her months ago—but it doesn't really matter. Tall, short, thin, lush, all I care about is how they tremble.

And if her demons might like mine.

I force myself to stay still. "Give it to me, or I'm not touching shit."

"Yes," she whispers against my callouses. They're so rough they could almost rip her pampered skin. The slick kiss of her mouth against my fingers makes me shudder. I want to shove them in deep—to watch her eyes water and feel her throat close and choke around them. "Fuck me. Fuck me hard. Fuck me, fuck me, fuck me plea—"

I shut her up with my tongue, taking her mouth hard.

Fuck yes, then.

She's sticky and tartly sweet, like sour candy. She gasps into my assault and melts into my chest. It's cute, but it's not what I want.

I want her to demand. To claw. To take. I want to earn my win. I want to see how hungry she is for it.

But her demons aren't like mine.

Still, her eager mouth tastes good, silky and wet, and plundering it feels like victory. Like a prize. The barbarian spoiling stolen royalty. I move one hand to her throat and push her back into the dirt until she's lying beneath me.

I want to split her thighs, to cover her nose and mouth and take until she screams in my ear, but she raises her arms up, crossing them at the wrists.

And . . . god damn it.

I know another dominant might get his panties wet over the seamless submission, but it kills some of my thrill to lean over her and use my cuffs on her the way she clearly wants. Only peacocks like Jasper use toys.

The kind of man who can't satisfy someone *without* extra help.

Shaking it off, I take her mouth again, harder, biting her

lower lip so she gives me another hot little gasp. When she arches under me, I tunnel my hands under her short dress, up her sleek thighs, and clasp her naked ass. I can feel the scorching, wet heat of her bare cunt through my jeans, and I grind my dick against her, rubbing her clit against the rough, punishing fabric. She whimpers, her breaths coming harshly, her pupils dark and blown. Above her head, her manicured fingers claw the dirt.

I bring my mouth down her throat, sucking and biting, my hands kneading her ass as I fuck her into the ground. Impatient to feel her, I pull back and yank down my zipper, then painfully tug my throbbing cock free. Need bites at me, but I force my hand steady as I slide on a condom, giving myself a few rough strokes while I do.

Alice stays put, trembling and red-cheeked. Her fingers twitch like she wants to move, to touch, and I want her to do it. To shove her awkward, cuffed hands between her legs and try to get some relief for that needy clit. To beg and demand and touch herself everywhere she wants to be touched while I jack myself off over her.

. . . But she holds herself back.

Again.

I grab one of her knees and wrench it wide, pulling her legs apart. "Open your legs."

She spreads them, and her dress falls back so I can see the wet tease of blonde curls over her cunt. I grip my cock. It throbs in my fist, and I squeeze it hard enough to hurt. I'm about to take her when she arches her calves prettily—in some fancy, studied move that instantly annoys the shit out of me.

I glower. "Stop that."

"W-what?" she asks uncertainly.

With a grunt, I let go of my cock, and with both hands,

yank her legs as wide as they'll go. Until the pretty arch disappears. Until her knees are pinned to the earth, and she's straining and stretched to her limits. I fill the space between her plush, round thighs, covering her with my heavy body and rubbing my dick against her scorching, slick folds. They part for me, and I grind down hard against her clit, back and forth, then round in tight, vicious circles. She lets out a raw, choked sound, then bites down hard on her lower lip, turning her face away. Her shiny blonde hair is splayed under her.

Getting dirty.

Getting *wrecked*.

Her unfiltered pleasure shudders through me and pressure builds at the base of my spine as I rut against her. I bury my face in her neck and growl against her. I nip her skin, and when she clutches at me, I bite her harder.

"Stop *pretending*." I thrust against her again, roughly, sloppily, just doing whatever feels good, the way I wish *she* would, too, and she cries out.

I feel her wetness coating my balls. The heat of her is everywhere. She still smells too fancy, and I rub her hair into the dirt, getting some fucked up pleasure out of bringing her down into the grime with me. Making her be *real*.

Her hips rock up against me, moving for the first time, pushing me where she wants me. Hesitant to start, then more bold. The green in her eyes hazes, and those neon red lights turn her infernal. Her cuffed wrists come up, hooking around my neck as she writhes into me, panting into my ear, and we're pressed so close now that I can feel her every shake and shiver.

"Oh." The word is strangled. Shocked. "*Oh, shit!*"

She wraps her legs around me, straining to get me inside her. Her scent is dizzying. Her pants lose rhythm, becoming wild, punctured by little whines and throaty whimpers that make me leak precum.

"Fuck." I turn her face and take her mouth again, drinking in her little cries, then pull down her dress. Her pale breasts are tipped with tight, pink peaks, and I drag my wet mouth across her flesh, leaving blooming red streaks where I suck and scrape and nip. I draw a nipple into my mouth, edging it with my teeth.

"Please, sir," she sobs. "*Please.*"

The *sir* throws me out again—I hate the formality, the distance—but she begins to tremble, and with a curse, I grasp my dick at the root and line myself with her entrance.

"Don't come without me," I snap. We can do round two back at the club, but for now, she's coming on my cock.

I shove into her, and her cunt is all dripping wet, searing heat. I cover her with my body, pressing us down into the earth, pressing us together until we're grinding against each other in a rough, rhythmless fury. Her pussy tightens around me, pulsing, and I pull back and fuck madly into her, taking whatever pleasure I can while she comes apart. Open. Free. Tears make helpless makeup tracks down her cheeks, and I press an openmouthed kiss against them. I lick the salt, and groan. My balls tighten. I'm slick with sweat, and she's soft and needy, and I bite down on her shoulder as I come hard.

She's still shaking when my brain starts functioning again, so I nuzzle against her, pressing kisses over every mark and bite I gave her until our breathing finally evens out. All that restless, itchy frustration settles, the weirdness in the air is forgotten, and slow satisfaction slides over me.

Fuck if these hunts aren't worth paying a massive slice of my salary in Darkside's membership fees.

Alice pulls back, and I slip out of her as she lifts her wrists back over my head. Realizing she's still cuffed, I free her, sneaking looks at her mascara-smeared face. Her eyes are wet with tears, her too-shiny hair now thoroughly roughed up. She looks dazed and a little shocked.

That look almost gets me off all over again.

Smugness makes its way into a smirk I can't help. It's good in the most fundamental way knowing I gave her what she needed. What we both needed.

I pause for a second as I watch her.

She *is* real pretty. My marks don't seem to suit her skin, not really, but there's potential.

Alice always seemed too lofty. Too posh and distant for me to bother looking twice. I'm not thick. I know how it goes with girls like her and guys like me.

But seeing her now, all dirt-spoiled and spent, I wonder if it could be different. Maybe if I tried. Maybe if I was a little less *me* and she was a little less *her*, we could be . . . I don't even know. Something.

It'd be nice to have more than nothing.

"So. You good?" As soon as the words are out of my mouth, I scowl. I sound like a fucking ape. I rub the back of my neck. "I mean, are you okay?"

Should I cuddle her? I don't usually bother unless they ask, and it's usually an awkward experience for both of us. But that's what people do, right? It's like flirting or whatever.

I'm debating how to go in for it without body slamming her when Alice blinks a few times, like she's coming back to herself. Color rushes into her cheeks, and I watch the flood of pink with a weird, jittery fascination. She pulls back a bit, then adjusts the skewed straps of her dress, putting those pretty tits away.

Realizing my arms are raised over my head like King Kong getting ready to swipe at a plane, I yank them back down.

Nope. Not hugging her. Not even gonna try.

My cheeks get hot as she shuffles her feet. I hope she didn't notice that. God damn it. How *do* people do this shit?

"I'm fine . . . thank you," she says. Politely. Like she doesn't have my bite marks up and down her neck. She gives me a tiny, reassuring smile, but she doesn't quite meet my eyes.

I stifle a frown, and distance floats between us again like cold air. As I watch her adjust the hem of her dress, I fidget awkwardly.

It might be . . . fine . . . to do this again. With the same person. It's been a long ass time since I've had more than a one-night stand. There never seemed like much point when I get deployed every other month—more and more often over the last few years. Not when I could catch bullets on any tour. Never seemed fair to make some poor girl have to dress up for my sorry ass funeral.

If anyone would even stick around long enough to bother.

But my chest tightens when I think about my trailer, tightens with something that gets closer to real panic every time I have to go home. I don't know how much longer I can take that silence.

Someone like Alice, though—I eye her as she examines a strand of filthy hair and grimaces—I bet she could help me pick out some of that frilly, pointless stuff that people always cram into their houses. Homey things.

Alice might fill out the space nice.

"Do you—" I cut off when she stands, and I put my dick away and get to my feet too, my tongue feeling thick and clumsy in my mouth. Nerves fritter over my skin. "I mean, would you want to do something sometime? With me? Do a thing together. Or whatever."

Her head whips back around, and she stares at me again.

I stare at her.

I kind of want to vomit. Why does this feel riskier than raiding a nuclear storage facility?

"Like . . . a date?" she asks hesitantly.

My shoulders hunch, and I don't know how to make them stop. " . . . Yeah?"

Her brows fly toward her hairline. "Oh."

Oh? What the hell does "oh" mean? I force myself to stop scowling.

The silence stretches, and the awkwardness feels like it's peeling my skin off. The heat in my cheeks roasts me.

I cross my arms over my chest.

I don't feel like a hunter anymore. I feel like a god damned voice-cracking teenager.

"Never mind," I mutter. "Stupid idea. I—"

"No. I mean, I just . . ." She shakes her head, still looking at me like I'm an escaped zoo animal. An odd one. Possibly dangerous. "I just don't think we'd have much in common. That's all."

My stomach drops into a pool of hot, bitter acid.

"Not much in common," I repeat slowly.

Alice bites her lip. "Well. Yes? I've been accepted to practice at Halifact and Slade. I'll be so busy there. And it involves all kinds of conferences and gala dinners, and I'm sure that would be so boring for you."

I watch her stutter over her words. The acid eats its way through my intestines, up my esophagus. It pools in my hollow chest.

"Boring for me." My lips twist. "Why would it be boring for me?"

Just let it go, Jayk. I'm being an asshole. It sounds boring as hell.

But the night has me on edge, the thought of my hollow trailer is squeezing the nauseous fluid in my chest . . . and I want her to admit it. That she thinks I'm too stupid to keep up with her. Too rough to try. That if I had a trust fund the size of the Grand Canyon, and if I manicured my ugly, tattered hands, then she wouldn't be saying this right now.

At my tone, a few tears spring into her eyes, and her hands knot in front of her. "I mean, wouldn't you rather be out playing pool or having beer with your friends?"

I hate pool.

And beer makes me gassy.

At least she didn't say dealing drugs or popping caps.

Rubbing a hand over my jaw, I can't help a cynical snort. I knew better than this. Girls like her and guys like me. I'm nothing but callouses and a fat dick to her.

"I'm sorry," she whispers. "We just have nothing in common."

"Yeah. Sure. Except going on hunts through fake ass floral gardens where you come hard enough to see stars." *Stop, asshole.* The sneer comes to my face anyway. "Except I'm the one who could get you to finally stop faking it for the first time in your life. No one looks that shocked to get off unless it's a rare event. You're welcome, by the way."

Good enough to play in the dirt with.

Good enough to leave there.

Alice's shoulders stiffen and color makes spots in her cheeks. "I think I should go."

Hearing the quaver in her voice, I look at her properly, seeing the tremble in her lips and the glassiness in her eyes.

Fuck.

Suddenly, all of that bitterness turns inward, and in one blistering second, I hate myself.

She's right. She's too good for me. Too clever. Too pretty. Too soft. And she didn't do a damn thing wrong.

I *am* the piece of shit here.

I made her *cry*.

I grip the back of my head. "Sorry," I mutter. "You . . . yeah. You're right. Do you need help—"

Lowlife. There's a reason my trailer's empty.

Alice shakes her head, avoiding my eyes again. "No. I know the way."

Torn between wanting to make sure she gets in okay and needing to kick something, I give a stiff nod. "Yeah. Sure."

There are Darkside monitors all through these gardens, and we really aren't that far from the club.

I spend a minute letting my stomach bile eat at me like acid, but just before she disappears into the trees, I scrub my hand over my face and call out, "Alice."

She hesitates, turning just a bit.

My throat feels raw. "Congratulations, you know? On Halifact and Slade. I'm sure you'll make a great lawyer."

Alice stares at me, then her face softens, and she nods at me once before vanishing.

I'm still standing there minutes later, wondering if I should book a hotel for the night rather than go back home, when a thick shoulder presses against mine.

Dom.

I close my eyes and grit my teeth. Why is he *still* here?

"You find flowers especially fascinating?" he asks dryly. "You don't strike me as a petunia guy."

I shove away from him. How much of that did he see? I cringe. All of it. Of course he saw fucking all of it.

Dom crosses his arms over his chest, studying me, and I glare at him. "*What*? If you have a problem, *Captain*, then just get it out."

He doesn't say anything, just keeps watching me, and I scowl, rolling my shoulders.

"What? You're pissed I made a subbie cry? That I piled all my shit on her right after a heavy scene rather than taking care of her?" *Worthless, stupid asshole.* "Or let me guess. You think I'm a dumb bastard for thinking I had a chance in hell with a girl like that to begin with?"

I want Dom to take a swing at me. Bad. I could use a fight, but I know better than to make the first hit on my CO, off duty or not.

But he doesn't bite. Instead, he rubs a hand over his jaw. Shaking his head, he says, "Doesn't sound like I need to."

I scoff, but he grabs my arm as I move to shove past him.

"I didn't say it, and I wouldn't, Jayk. You're a good man. Fucking up after that scene notwithstanding."

Yeah. Right.

Good men don't make nice girls cry.

Dom releases me gingerly, then shrugs one shoulder. "She just turned you down, man. It happens."

I glare at him. "I could give a shit that she turned me down. She can do what she wants."

And I hate the way he tilts his head to consider me. It's how he looks at subbies. Slowly, he nods. "It's *why* she turned you down." He grimaces. "Look, Jayk—"

"Thanks for the session, Dr. Phil." I sneer. "But I already have one pompous shrink trying to hold my hand. How 'bout you stick to running drills and keeping us out of heavy fire and leave the emotional jacking off to him?"

Jasper might have retired, but he still keeps calling to "check in." Some days, I even answer.

Dom rolls his eyes. "If you want to do drills, I can have you back on base at oh-six-hundred. I'll run you down until you beg Beau for an oxygen mask."

When I glower at him, he sighs. "Alice is great, but she's set in her world. The things she wants. You'd be like a bomb on her life. Or are you trying to tell me that you'd go along to cocktail hour and make nice while the good old boys chat about the latest stock fluctuations?"

"I could do the boyfriend shit," I mutter.

Could I? Just the idea of "good old boys" makes me want to start shit. But it has to beat coming home empty.

"Right. I'm sure you'd be great at . . . boyfriend shit." Dom's lips press like he's trying to hold in a smirk. "But maybe you should pick someone else? Someone who's into the same things you are?"

Someone in my lane, he means. Someone like me.

Maybe he's even right. But I sure as hell ain't going to find them at Darkside—not for thirty-thou-a-year membership fees. I could go back to some of the public clubs, but most of them are cesspits. And I can't help but think that if I did get with someone like me, someone who really understood all the shit that comes along with the life I've lived, that we'd drown in each other's bitterness.

I don't want someone like me.

Is it wrong to want someone gentle? Hopeful? I've seen so much shit. It'd be nice to be with someone . . . kind.

But that's the stupid curse of this life. Anyone like that is going to be like Alice, and they're going to run as far and fast away from me as they can.

Dom's still looking at me expectantly, but all that's too far down touchy-feely lane. It's not like we're *friends*. Not the real kind, anyway. Not the kind that shares shit. I doubt he even knows Ryan's name.

So I shrug noncommittally. "Yeah. Maybe."

The captain looks me over, then claps my shoulder and starts walking towards the club. I follow after him.

"You know," he calls back. "If you really want to do all of that 'boyfriend shit,' you should ditch that trailer. Actually get a nice place. Women usually like having a real home to go to."

My steps slow for a second as the casual, wry words hit me in the gut. Dom has no clue. Doesn't get that a double wide even could be a 'real home.' I fucking hate that trailer . . . but it *is* my home. My mom raised me there. She lived there, got sick there, died there. My brother and I crashed there between tours, before the accident. It's still my home, even if everyone who made it one is dead. Out of our squad, Lucky's the only one who's even seen it.

I whack a branch out of my face so hard it snaps. "Whatever. You can go back to keeping your nose out of my shit anytime."

I pull up beside him as we approach Darkside.

Dom rolls his eyes at me. "Give me a break. Beau's been gone a week. I swear, his mom's going to tempt him out of the Rangers with cherry pies alone."

"He back soon?" My question's distracted. With the adrenaline and drama fading, that off feeling is coming back, and harder than it has all day. A chill races up my spine, and the hairs on my arms start lifting up. It's like the air is made of electric prickles.

It feels like we're about to get zapped.

Even the captain seems to sense it this time, frowning at the brightly lit club. "Any day. Depends how much Beth, Brooke and Bailey drive him up the wall."

I grunt. I've met the medic's sisters—they're bossy, nosy, and *chatty*. I don't care how good Mama Bennett's pies are, they're not worth it.

Both of us pause.

"The lights are on," Dom murmurs.

Not the party lights, or the scene lights. Fluorescent, obnoxious, time-to-go-home lights. Except it's only eleven, and those lights only go on at three in the morning.

Uneasiness settles over me. "They cut the music."

Dom checks his radio, and the green light blinks up at us. No one's contacted him.

"Probably some club drama. Some rookie not checking their ropes." Medical emergencies aren't common—Darkside has monitors and mandatory safety courses for a reason—but shit happens.

"Hm." His frown deepening, Dom gestures at me to move in behind and cover him, and he strides inside. Out of habit, more than anything, I follow his lead.

The first two rooms are a ghost town—I've never seen them that empty—and we follow the rising crash of voices from the massive presentation room. There are too many people packed into this one space, all of them staring up at the huge triple screens above the main bar.

And this is it. I know it is. And it's almost a relief, for the shoe to drop. It's not head doctor shit. Something's gone down.

From this angle, I can't see the screens, but their faces . . .

My relief fades, and my stomach turns—because their faces tell me this isn't regular bad. Not "called out to avert disaster" bad, or "near miss" bad.

From their faces, this was a direct hit.

From their faces . . . it looks like the world just fucking ended.

EPISODE TWO

DOMINIC

Naval Base Kitsap. Whiteman Air Force Base. Camp David..."

Jayk's right on my heels as I storm inside, already pulling out my satellite phone. The familiar names crawl out of the speakers in a dead, droning recitation. Around the room, every face is bone white and wide-eyed as they stare and stare.

I'm braced for the strike, but the words "EMERGENCY BROADCAST SYSTEM" still catch me under the ribs.

Jayk snorts as he eyes my phone, though the set of his jaw is grim. "You kept the sat phone? Colonel Daddy will have your ass."

"Who do you think told me to take it?"

"...*Jim Creek Naval Radio Station*..."

I hit speed dial on my old man's number, my gut tightening. They haven't listed our base yet, so there's a chance it's fine. There are plenty of locations they'll want to hit before ours—it might not be on the strike list at all, depending on how many warheads were mobilized. This is bad, but we can fix it. We'll get our orders, get loaded up, and we'll get on this thing.

The call rings out.

"*Fuck!*"

I glare down at the screen to see thirteen voicemails. I've only been at the club for a few hours. They're recent.

I open the first message from an unknown number.

> This is a message from the Federal Emergency Management Agency: nuclear detonations have occurred in multiple locations across the country. To protect yourself and your family, get inside, stay inside, and stay tuned for more information. Move to the lowest level and most interior portion of the building if possible. Follow instructions from officials—this can save your life. Martial law is now in place.

My head starts to pound, but it's my war drum. It focuses me. That sharp, bursting adrenaline—that *fear*—strips away all the messy thoughts and leaves only the problem.

If this is what I think it is, then our asses need to get into gear fast.

"...*VLF Transmitter Cutler*..."

"What are we doing? Are we heading back to base?" Lucky pops up beside my shoulder like a whack-a-mole, buckling his belt. His cheeks are flushed, his eyes a little glassy. He's been riding a high, and he's still coming down.

Of the 75th Ranger Regiment, we only have Third Battalion currently at our base, and of my company—Delta Company—only Jayk, Lucky, and Thomas are here at the club. The rest are either on base or off duty as well, and none of our off-duty guys have sat phones. No way for me to contact them. That thought stutters through my focus.

Beau doesn't have a sat phone.

The war drum in my head grows louder, but it struggles to beat the new worry down.

"... *Houston. Atlanta. Los Angeles...*"

Lucky freezes, then his head snaps up to the screen.

Fuck.

His family is from Los Angeles.

Sympathy bites at me, but I smother it. We're not grieving today. This is an active situation, and we're not wasting time worrying about things we can't change. He needs to hurt over this later.

"Lock it down, Lucky."

I clap his shoulder and squeeze it to soften the words, but I find my eyes drifting back up to the emergency broadcast as the names keep coming through the speakers in quick-fire blows. I've seen a lot of shit since I enlisted, but this is different.

"... *Kings Bay Naval Base...*"

Uppercut.

"... *Kirtland Air Force Base...*"

Kidney shot.

"... *Washington D.C....*"

A scream rips apart the stricken silence, and the crowd bursts apart like a flock startled into flight.

Hallie backs up, her play bag hanging off one shoulder. "*No.* My brother— He just had a baby. I can't ..."

She looks at me, and her lips are bloodless. Hallie's a domme. Been at the club for longer than I have. Beau tried to flirt with her on our first day and she threatened to lock him in a cock cage if he couldn't keep it in his pants. Hallie doesn't take shit, and she's not easy to ruffle.

Beau had better be okay. He's with his parents—his whole

family are together for Brooke's birthday. No, they're okay. They're far enough out from major cities. They'll be okay.

"They're hitting cities, too?"

"Is your phone working?"

"No signal."

"My brother is in Washington!"

"The radio just has the same message."

"This is a joke, right? Like a War of the Worlds thing?"

Reception is spotty in the club. It's too remote for reliable coverage, but suddenly there are dozens of screens flashing around the room. Everyone's dialing and clutching their cells to their faces like they're oxygen masks and no one's catching air. The hum of the crowd rises to a frantic pitch and it's hard to make out the broadcast.

"Cell network's out," Jayk mutters, sounding resigned. He checks his phone. "Internet too."

No shit. They were always going to be an early target. This sat phone will be worth its weight in gold soon, even if it'll only connect to other sat phones.

Even though it *won't* connect me to Beau.

God damn it. He'll go back to base. He's not an idiot. He'll meet us there.

"I heard Los Angeles." Jasper strides up, anxiously stroking the vicious blacksnake secured at his hip. His eyes are locked on Lucky, and the small lines at their corners are deep and tense.

I'd heard Jasper was roped into giving a whipping demonstration tonight, but it's still a surprise to see him. He's been AWOL since he retired as our shrink six months ago—at the tender age of thirty-eight, not that we're allowed to question *that* fucking fact.

"I'm so sorry, Lucien," Jasper says softly.

Lucky blinks, a small frown marring his forehead. He tears his gaze away from the broadcast and looks at Jasper, his face pale and his blue eyes blown dark.

Hugh, one of the subs who had been in the hunt, shoves off his dom and throws his phone to the side with a vicious, choked curse. Thomas comes up beside them, talking with coaxing hands. Someone storms past him, toward the door, and he throws me an urgent look, wanting orders.

I slash a hand signal at him. *Deal with it.*

Someone starts crying behind me, and the war drum *beats, beats, beats* in my head.

"Everyone stay put!" I bellow, and a handful of civs skitter away from me.

Sure, like *I'm* what they need to be scared of right now. I glare at them, and uneasiness grips my gut when more people head to the doors.

I flick through my voicemails quickly, opening the last one from the colonel.

From my dad.

"Captain Slade, we have Code Alpha. Martial law is in place, and it's already a shitshow out there, so prioritize speed. Bring civs if you have to but I need your team back at base yesterday. This is going to get rough." There's a pause, and my dad's voice turns gruff. "Mentally alert, physically strong, and morally straight, son. Rangers lead the way."

There's a beat of silence as I stare at my phone.

"Well ain't that cute. You two ever speak normally? Or do you just recite the fucking creed back at each other and call it a day?" Jayk's voice is too shaky to hold the snark, and he's staring at my phone like it just bit him.

Of course he's rattled. You don't hear Code Alpha and not

be ready to shit your pants, I don't care how trained you are. Code Alpha isn't life changing.

It's world shattering.

"...*NORAD Peterson Space Force Base*..."

I fucking knew it. This isn't a broadcast. It's an obituary.

Gritting my teeth, I hit the speed dial again, but nothing.

My thumb strokes over the screen as I tuck the phone away and ignore Jayk. He doesn't get it; his dad is a piece of shit. Mine might be one of the few people who can pull our asses out of this fire. I don't need him to write me a poem. I need him to do his job, just like he needs us to do ours.

I fix our group with a hard look. "We need to get these civs mobile. If they wander into a blast site looking for their families, they're dead. We need to take control of this. Are you good?"

Lucky's bruised eyes are still on Jasper. "I'm fine."

"You're not fine, Lucien," Jasper scolds, and I shoot him an impatient glare. He can save the tender loving shit for later.

The tendons in Lucky's throat grow taut, but a forced smile tugs his lips up on one side. "Don't worry about it. My parents were just talking about hitting the road. I doubt they're even there. I'm good. You want me to take the door? How are we doing this?"

"...*Strategic Command, Offutt Air Force Base*..."

Fuck. That one's a big problem. That, with the others? That's our highest order decision-making gone. My old man really is going to need backup.

There's a loud crash. Damn it, someone's rifling through the bar.

Distracted, urgency beating through me, I eye Lucky. His folks are always talking about traveling. Starting up with a mobile show.

As far as I know, they've never even left California.

Jasper shakes his head. "Perhaps we should—"

"He said he's fine, Jasper." I wait until Lucky glances at me, then hold his gaze. "His folks are traveling."

The look Jasper gives me is frigid. Lethal.

I ignore him. "Lucky, get Thomas and take the door. Don't let anyone leave. Jayk, you're backup. I'm about to give these folks some shitty news."

Lucky rolls his shoulders, and I see him switch from civ to soldier. "You want me to stop people leaving?" One brow kicks up. "You sure about that, Cap?"

Nope.

Beau would be my usual compass check on shit like this.

But Beau isn't fucking *here*.

"They can't go off half-cocked looking for their people," I say instead, as the drum becomes a sledgehammer inside my skull. "We get them to an evacuation zone or back to base. They don't get a choice. Not this time. I'll knot them in every rope we have here and haul them out if I need to."

"... *Minot Air Force Base* ..."

Jasper sighs beside me. "Fine, Dominic. What would you have me do?"

Jasper? I look at him in surprise. What *can* Jasper do? I respect his work, but it means nothing to me in this situation. Still, he's keeping his head. He's not begging me to try to call his parents.

Or his wife.

"Help Jaykob," I say vaguely, already turning toward the wide bar. Braydon freezes, his hand still gripping the vodka. He has two more bottles under his arm, but I ignore him, climbing up onto the polished wood until I'm standing under the emergency broadcast screens.

No one looks up.

Jaykob and Jasper position themselves by my feet, and Thomas nods at me from the front door, manning it with Lucky.

Between me and them, the crowd swarms like panicked ants. Cries and snippets of anxious conversations pummel me.

"Did you hear Boston? I have a second home in Boston, maybe I can go there."

"Are we getting invaded?"

"Do you think it was—"

I put the whistle I had for the hunt between my lips and blow. The piercing shriek cuts through the room over and over until I finally get eyes on me.

"I need you all to shut up and listen," I snap.

"Easy," Jasper murmurs, and I try not to grind my teeth.

They're not soldiers, but they *are* subbies. Doms.

They can take some damn orders.

" . . . *VLF Transmitter Lualualei* . . ."

"Most of you know me as Master Dom, but outside Darkside, I'm Captain Slade, head of Delta Company in the 75th Ranger Regiment of the United States Army Special Operations Command."

I look over the stressed faces staring up at me. I know most of them. I've *dommed* some of them.

With *Beau*.

"We've been hit in multiple locations and have no intel at this stage of where, or if, we might be hit next. Everyone pack your things. Make sure you have transportable water, warm clothes, blankets, and whatever food, tools, and weapons you can find. We're going to the evacuation center near our base—our people will take care of you there."

Silence.

Done. I bend to get down when they surge forward.

"The hell I'm going anywhere with you. My daughter is at home!"

"Can you really keep us safe?"

"The emergency message said to stay inside and wait for instructions."

" . . . *Malmstrom Air Force Base* . . ."

Fuck fuck *fuck*. Why is the public prep around a ballistic attack so fucking non-existent?

I blow my whistle again, but only half of them are paying attention to me now. People are turning, crowding Lucky and Thomas.

"These *are* your instructions," I thunder down at them. They have to hear me on this. This is life or death for them. "The nearest city is hours away. We had no physical sign of a disturbance here. We're most likely outside a fallout zone, and we don't have the supplies to go to ground here. We move while we can—and we stay *out* of those strike locations. If your people were there, then they're either dead or they need to find their own way. The sooner you accept that, the more likely you are to survive."

Jasper sighs, then mutters, "Very tactful."

Jason, a big dom I've had over for barbecue before, flips me off. "Go fuck yourself, Dom, how about that?"

"You need to start *thinking*, asshole," I snap back.

The crowd surges again, and someone lunges at Lucky. Thomas covers him, tossing the guy back easily, but two more fill his place.

Damn it, they're not listening. Why aren't they *listening*? Don't they have any sense of self-preservation? They need to switch it off.

Uncertainty eats at my resolve as Lucky grimaces, pushing Greg back. He's fucked Greg before. He's fucked Greg before and now he has to fight him?

Clusters are holding back. Pockets of people are crying. Some are angry. Some are gathering shit up like it's a fire sale. These people are scared shitless.

Lucky gives me a questioning look, his face red with strain.

Am I really prepared to use force against *civilians*, even to keep them safe? Martial law or not, this isn't sitting right. Beau would have a problem with this.

"You want me up front?" Jayk asks.

My stomach drops, and I hesitate. I linger on Hallie's red-rimmed eyes as she shoves at Thomas.

No. I'm not using force against these people. Darkside is all about choice, and they have the right to choose their fate. Even if it's stupid. Even if they're *emotional*. Something rips in me.

Even if it means their life.

"...*Robins Air Force Base*..."

Voices lift into a deafening shout, cutting off the last name, but my head snaps up anyway. I can't see the screen. I jump down and back up, though I know the image hasn't changed.

Blood pulses in my head, and the war drum staggers, loses its rhythm.

Not there. Robins is less than twenty miles from Mama Bennett's farm. With these nukes, that blast radius...

Jayk's hand grips my shoulder. "Hey, how far are we taking this? They're losing their shit."

My lips are numb. "They would have been fried."

Jayk gives me a strange look. The room is a whirling mix of color and sound.

Beau is dead.

"Lucien and Thomas are getting overwhelmed, Dominic. Make a decision. Now." Jasper's voice is cold. Curt.

I rub my forehead. Right. There's a problem here. We process later. We grieve *later*.

I try to think, but for some reason, Beau is in my head, grinning and flipping me off as he got into his truck. He held it outside the window as he drove off.

Clearing my throat, I manage, "The ones who want to go can leave. Tell them . . ."

I frown. I can't even remember what Beau flipped me off for.

"What happened? Why is he like this?"

"Fuck if I know. Shit, Thomas is down."

It was only three days ago. Why can't I *remember*?

"Enough," Jasper hisses.

Stepping forward, he uncoils the blacksnake from his forearm. He pivots away from the crowd. Lifting his arm in a villainous flourish, he snaps the whip in a cruel *crack* that thunders through the room. The crowd shrieks, rearing back, and he cracks it again.

"Lucien, move aside. Let them go," Jasper orders into the abrupt, shocked lull.

The room focuses enough for me to see Lucky's blond buzz cut catch the light as he drags a bleeding Thomas away from the door. I watch vaguely as dozens of people pour through the front door.

Dozens of people who are probably going to die.

Just like *Beau*.

I feel sick to my stomach. It's a cold, roiling nausea that's never hit me in an active situation before. But Beau is dead, and it doesn't make sense.

How can he be dead? He's the other half of my whole fucking soul. The *good* half. He can't just be *gone*.

Maybe two dozen people stay inside. There's too much shouting and crying, and we don't have time for it. I know that. You don't make captain by crying over every dead soldier, especially lately. Especially while things are still so hot. There's shit to do.

If Beau's dead, that's just bad fucking luck.

"We have to get supplies. Anything we can use," I say, looking up at Jayk and Jasper.

Only Jasper isn't here. He's over with Lucky, pressing a handkerchief against Thomas's bleeding brow.

When did he move?

Jayk is still staring at me.

"Are you deaf? We need supplies." I shoulder past him, not sure where I'm going.

My war drum is gone, and I've lost my rhythm, but I don't need it. I'll figure it out. It's what I'm trained for.

The rest of the room is still so dizzy and too fucking loud, but I see one of the subbies curled up under the bar. Curled up like the small lip of wood will protect him. His black-painted nails are buried in his blue hair and sobs wrack his body.

He's still got his purple newbie band.

My own throat burns.

"Don't cry about it. Get up," I tell him roughly, my voice coming out too thick.

The kid curls in tighter on himself, and I kneel down beside him. I'm not failing this one too. There won't be any more obituaries walking out that door. "Come on, kid. I don't get to cry about it, you don't get to cry. We act. We *move*."

I remember my dad telling me that.

I can do this. Mentally alert, physically strong, morally straight. Rangers lead the way. I can *do* this.

Someone hauls me back by my collar, and I swing around fists first, adrenaline snapping through me. Jayk grunts as my knuckles collide with his thick abs, but he keeps dragging me with him, and I stop fighting him. It's only Jayk. I do curse him all the way out the door, though.

He throws me into the now almost deserted parking lot.

"What the fuck was that?" Gravel crunches under my feet and the night breeze catches against my cheeks. My wet cheeks.

I bring a hand up to touch one, and my calluses are rough over the dampness.

Why can't I remember why Beau flipped me off?

Jayk crosses heavy, tatted arms over his chest. His dark blue eyes are almost black in the midnight shadows.

Out here, the night's silence is suffocating.

"Do you think he felt it?" I whisper.

He frowns at me. "Who felt what?"

Something drips off my chin.

"Do you think Beau felt it when he got nuked?" Beau's a baby about burns. He bitched for a week when he scalded his tongue.

Radiation's meant to burn. Bad.

I grip the back of my neck, and my breath comes in trembling. "I really hope he didn't feel it, you know?"

"Beau was caught in it?" Jayk asks sharply, but I don't think I can answer. It's suddenly hard to breathe.

I bend over and brace my hands on my knees as everything spins.

Jayk is silent for a long minute. "We'll get the civs ready to move, Dom. Just . . . take a beat. Come back in when your head's straight." His voice is heavy, and softer than I'm used to when he adds, "Cry about it. You get to."

I hear the crunch as he walks away, and my chest heaves. I think it splits in two. I don't know how to do this. Take a minute? What the fuck is a minute going to do? He's my whole life.

The road swirls under me.

What will I do with our apartment? It's too big for one person, and he has so much shit there. Beau's a goddamned hoarder. He likes knickknacks. Nobody likes knickknacks before they're eighty.

My shoulders start shaking, and I sit my ass in the gravel before I fall over. The moon glazes everything a hot, blurry silver. I squeeze a hand over my face but it does nothing.

An alpha strike wasn't meant to be possible—not here, not on *our* turf. It's the whole reason we do this fucking job. I know it's been getting worse, so much goddamn worse, but the level of coordination, the infrastructure, the fucking *balls* . . . it shouldn't have been possible.

I've lost soldier after soldier these last five years, but Beau's been at my side for every funeral. Every time we talk to their mamas after. It's him I tip to every time we drink in their memory.

There's not enough booze in the world to honor Beau.

I wrap into myself and cry.

A car starts rolling up toward Darkside, and I only bother to look up when it parks right in front of me. Here and now, this remote? It's only going to be another member. A civ from earlier changing their mind, maybe.

But when I see the cherry red pickup, I decide I'm hallucinating.

Slowly, I get to my feet, staring. I'm half-frozen, like someone's about to swing a camera in front of my face and call it all off as a shitty joke.

The driver-side window rolls down.

". . . Beau?" I say shakily.

He waves his hand at me but doesn't look over. "Shh, shh. Just keep your pie hole stuffed shut. I didn't take every backroad over Georgia today only to miss how this ends."

I follow his gaze to his phone, which he's plucked from the console beside him. His favorite podcast winks up at me —*Greatest Unsolved Mysteries: The Truths No One Wants You to Know.* He always downloads episodes when he's traveling.

Beau's tanned from days lounging on his mama's porch, loose and relaxed and clearly without a clue about what's gone down over the last few hours.

Because he's been listening to a fucking *podcast*?

" . . . and while science may never confirm what really happened that night, we at GUM believe these facts speak for themselves."

Beau claps his hand against the steering wheel. "They did it again! I really don't know how they keep convincing me science is bullshit and yet here we are. I *do* want to think the faeries took that whole town, Dom. So that's what I'm going to believe."

Every episode of that stupid podcast is a crime against rational thought.

"You haven't turned your radio on?" I say incredulously.

He's here. *Is* he here? Or did I just have an aneurysm?

Beau finally looks up at me, squinting against the moonlight. "Why would I listen to the radio? It's only got bad music or bad news, and I've got no time for that. The faeries, Dom. I had to know about the faeries."

"You haven't checked your *phone*?" I demand, my heart thundering. That emergency text went out two hours ago.

My eyes stick on every feature. Every hair and eyelash. Relief detonates inside me in bright, blinding light.

"You know I don't check my phone while I'm driving, Dom. It's not safe," he scolds, then tries to push the door open with a snort. "The signal never works out here anyway. Would you move? Why are you standing so close?"

When it opens, I smell apple pie and heat burns the backs of my eyes again. I grab Beau and yank him out of the car, pulling him into a fierce hug.

"Hey now, I missed you too, buddy," he says on a laugh, hugging me back.

I can't reply, so I just squeeze him tighter.

I know this thing between us is different. Weird enough to go on his stupid podcast, maybe. It's not something I've ever had the ability or interest to explain. I don't want to fuck him. I just want our lives to bleed together until we die.

Until we die *together*.

He doesn't get to do that without me.

These fucking tears leak out of me again.

"Dom? What is it? What's wrong?"

Worry scorches the humor out of his tone, and he eases back.

He studies my face. "Dom, are you . . .?" His voice hardens with fear. "You tell me what's happened right now."

I step back, shaking my head. Now my nausea is settling, a

different kind of panic rises. His face is more familiar than my own, and right now his gives me confusion. Unease. He doesn't *know*.

How can I tell him his family is dead?

Grief opens up in empty caverns and black holes inside me.

They were my family too.

"Why did you ask about my phone?" He pulls it out again, and it's the coward's way, but I don't have it in me to stop him.

I look away as he reads through the notification. The last one he would have received before comms went down.

"Dom, what is this?" There's a vulnerable thread through the question this time, and it makes me want to cry all over again.

This is going to break him. Beau loves big. His family loved like that too.

Thirty minutes ago, my responsibilities were everything. There are people inside that club who need me. These attacks could keep coming at any moment. We have a thousand things to do and plan and *be*. We never have time for these kinds of feelings.

But right now, all I want to do is handle Beau like an eggshell.

"It's a Code Alpha." Beau shakes his head, but I talk over the silent protest. "Colonel Slade called it—he's summoned us to base."

I never talk around hard truths. That's Beau's wheelhouse. I have to give it to him straight, I know I do, especially when he gives me that apprehensive look. I see the growing fear behind his eyes.

He knows me too well.

"Your family . . ." The rest clogs in my throat.

Beau pulls away from the words, his breathing unsteady, and I step in and grab the back of his neck, pressing our foreheads together. If he has to go through this, then he's doing it with me right here with him.

Maybe it'll only hurt half as much if we take the hurt together.

"Robins AFB was a target. It was hit with an ICBM at time unknown today, and it's on the official list of casualty locations from the most recent national broadcast."

Beau's eyes sink closed. "Stop, don't say it, Dom. Don't."

I don't want to. I'd give limbs to make it not true. But it is, and he has to know.

I hear the front door of the club swing open, and I know we've run out of time. A shitstorm is waiting for us out in the real world.

We all need to face reality now.

So I squeeze the back of Beau's neck like anything I do will make the next words hurt any less . . . and I blow up my best friend's world.

"They couldn't have made it, Beau. Your family is dead."

Episode Three
Beau

Dom's fingertips dig into my neck. His nails are trimmed, blunted, and his wide palm presses against my nape. I can feel the graze of every callus. He's real and grounding in a world that feels suddenly . . . strange.

The podcast is ringing in my ears, sending absurd images through my mind. Infernos and bursts of gunfire. The Bennett farm swallowed by faerie mists.

My hands shake against Dom's shirt.

It was Brooke's birthday yesterday. Bailey made a drunken punch out of peaches from Brooke's farm, and Dad sucked it down like a horse at a trough. He spent half the night pinching Mama's ass when he thought we weren't looking, and the other half staring at us all with a wet shine to his eyes.

That was just *hours* ago.

I can still taste the boozy peaches kicking me in the back of the teeth.

Dom's gaze is burnt honey, bitter and dark as he holds me against his forehead. The raw fluorescent lights are harsh, glaring into the midnight murk. They grind into the tired lines on his face and slash over his damp cheeks.

I can't do this.

His eyes are rubbed red, and I just *can't*. It's all unreal. Surreal.

But Dom . . . Dom is too real.

I wrench out of his grip, fumbling for the truck's handle, but my fingers are numb, and I can't get a grip on it. That's a symptom. Shock, most probably—or a stroke, but all considered, I'm guessing it's shock. I manage to get the door open, and the smell hits me like a slap to the face.

Cinnamon and apples.

I look over to the passenger seat. The apple pie stares at me, crisp and golden, the Saran wrap sweating because Mama packaged it up right out of the oven.

"Share it with your friends, hon, don't eat it all yourself. You're getting soft in the middle. Oh, what now? Don't you look at me like that, Beth, he's doughy! It don't make him any less handsome. Girls love a bit of pooch. Now, go on, hon. You give Dommie a kiss for me."

I'm frozen. The door's still cracked, and Dom pulls it wide open. "What are you doing?"

He's gentle, and the wrongness starts to suck the truck out from under me. Voices filter in around us, disembodied and wispish, and cars peel out of the parking lot with desperate, jarring screeches.

"I'm going to get them." I yank at the door.

Dom doesn't budge. "Can it with the truck, Beau. There's nothing for you there. Not anymore."

He's hard. Clipped.

Real.

The pie is real.

What he's saying is *real*.

Panic tramples me. I punch around and shove him back. "No. *No*. Don't you do this. They're our family, Dom."

He doesn't let me push him far. When I stagger, he grips my biceps and anchors me against the truck's frame, holding me like I'm ash that's about to crumple in his hands.

His red-rimmed eyes shine in the moonlight. "I know."

My pulse pounds. It's too fast, and my deep breath comes in shuddery. More symptoms I don't much care to do anything about right now.

"They need me." The broken whisper slips out like a plea.

Dom punches out a hard, harsh breath. "No, Beau. They don't."

Immediately, he flinches, like he didn't mean to say it. But he did. The weight of his words crushes the night air.

They don't need me.

They *don't* . . .

Dom's holding me up before I've realized I'm sagging, and I press my head against his chest. Black edges my vision. He turns his head, and his hard exhale breezes over my hair.

"I'm sorry, Beau." he whispers, and the choked edge to it makes my eyes burn. "I'm so fucking sorry."

The breeze whips us, and the frantic sounds are cut down in the swirl. It's going to spirit us off. It drags the haunted scent around.

Cinnamon and apples. Everything is cinnamon and apples.

It's just not right.

I *just* saw them.

I stagger back from Dom. Away from apple pie and my dead mama's voice.

"We have thirty. You ready to . . . Is that Beau?" Jayk stops hard in the doorway, staring at me while people crowd behind him. He pales, searching my face like it's not the world that's gone mad. He's looking at me like *I'm* strange. Like I just walked out of my family's grave.

I wonder if he can see their ash cloud at my back.

I shudder.

Mistress Hallie shoves Jayk out of the doorway, and he scowls down at her. When he turns back to me, his jaw flexes . . . and I can't help but think that he's the odd one. Relief is stark, naked on his face, and it doesn't fit him. Jayk is all insults and bad attitude. He doesn't worry about any of us. I don't care how many times he's covered my ass. He's just my co-worker. On a *good* day, he's my co-worker.

He's not my family.

Jayk stares at me a minute more, then nods to me once.

Unnerved, I look up at the sky, and it all swirls away again. There are words, *sounds*—Dom barking orders, Jayk growling impatiently as the civilians flood out of Darkside—but they're airy and insubstantial.

Swallowing, I shudder. How did this happen?

I turn back to my pickup, and the pie stares back at me.

Cinnamon and apples.

"Oh, darlin', really? You have to go already? Next time just bring Dommie with you so you don't have to rush back. You know I get heartsick every time you leave."

Dom's wide hand comes down on my shoulder. He turns me sharply, his brows slamming down. "Beau . . . you hearing me? Can you . . . "

White noise.

Slowly, I blink at him, then I breathe in more fresh-baked home. My mama pats my cheek after I kiss her goodbye.

Painfully, I pull free of Dom's grip. I walk over to the truck and slam the driver-side door shut.

The sweet, wafting scent dies.

I lean back against the truck, closing my eyes.

"Beau? *Beau*. Fuck." Dom's voice lifts. "Okay, everyone, we're starting a convoy. Beau and I are taking point. Jayk and Thomas, you're center. Lucky, pull up the rear. We're heading for the Howards Evacuation Center. It's about thirty miles outside of base. Load up your cars, we're heading out in ten. Jayk, Lucky, Thomas, here."

I breathe out, slowly, trying to soothe my jumbled thoughts, and the air floats through my body like it's not even there.

I was listening to a *podcast*.

The urge to get back in my truck and drive home has me by the throat.

But *they don't need me.*

My hands shake.

How can they not need me? Bailey was tearing me a new one just yesterday for not visiting more. Last year, I was deployed ten months out of twelve. They do need me—and I haven't *been here*.

No. It's just not right. The world doesn't just *end*. It's a ghost story, a spook, a boogeyman. Brooke used to tease me with nightmares until I wept like a baby, and way older than I'm proud to admit. Beth used to let me hide in her room and didn't say a single word on it. This is like that. That's all it is. It *can't* be real.

It's too . . . big.

Other memories start flicking through my brain like flipping pages. Shutting down that nuclear facility in the freezing ass crack of winter. Assault op after assault op. The bodies, ripped apart by gunfire, laid out on dusty floors. Tile. Blood-stained snow. The full regiment hitting two airfields that were so loaded up, they could have wiped out the west coast. The rumors of SEAL deployments, Berets, of everyone *moving*. It's been tense. Hot. No one's far from their phones.

A chill skates down my spine as the wind buffets me against the truck.

The weapons we've destroyed line themselves up in my mind.

That one for Bailey.

That one for Brooke.

Beth.

My dad.

My mom.

The next breath I suck in nearly guts me.

It's all too big . . . but that doesn't mean it's not true.

"Does *anyone* have reception? *Please*." A woman sobs, and I try to control my shivers.

God, how could it all be for nothing? How many did we *miss*?

I trusted our bloody, awful work. I trusted there was a reason. I trusted our government. Our people. This was all meant to keep *my* people safe.

But now?

What was it all for?

" . . . in the truck?"

I lift my head, numb. Dom, Jayk, Lucky, Thomas, and, strangely, Jasper, are gathered around. Thomas grimaces, avoiding my eyes, and Dom's mouth is a tense line. He's watching me like he's waiting for an answer.

I didn't even realize he'd been talking.

"Gear, Beau. What are you packing?" He's brusque, all captain again.

I shake my head.

"Rifle? Bug out bag?"

It's a muddy night. Looking up, I can't see a single star, just cloud after cloud. Too many souls stuck in the sky.

Dom blows out an impatient breath. "Beau, do you have—"

"I was going home, Dom. I don't have . . ." I have one duffel, packed with clothes my mama washed and ironed for me before I left. Because I might be thirty years old, but there's no way she could ever let me leave with un-ironed boxer briefs. "I have my pistol. My uniform . . ." My throat sticks. My dad's hand clasps my wrist as he hugs me goodbye. "I was going home."

The clouds press together, choking out the night.

Car doors open and close. Civilians shout at each other. So much noise.

I just want to go home.

There's a tense silence around our circle, and then Jasper clears his throat. He drops the anxious hand from his forehead and sighs. "I have most of my remaining belongings packed in my car. I was intending to drive to my summer home, Bristle-brook, in the morning. There may be some useful items in there, but you will likely be a better judge of that. I believe I have a first aid kit." He gives Dom a stiff smile. "Though no firearms, I'm afraid."

Lucky looks up from his rifle, startled. "Wait, you're moving?"

Jasper tenses, then lifts his brows, cool and distant in a silent *yes, and?*

Thomas clears his throat loudly, and Dom smacks the back of his head.

Lucky glances at them, shifting. The gravel crunches under his feet. "I— You weren't even going to say goodbye?"

The silence is deafening. A low, heavy ache cramps my stomach.

When the awkward silence stretches too long, Lucky lets out a strangled, casual laugh. "To say goodbye to . . . to any of us, I mean. You weren't going to . . . You didn't have a going away party, or anything. I— Why are you leaving? Is . . . is Soomin going with you?" Suddenly, his face turns deathly white. "Oh, *fuck*, Jasper. Soomin. We need to go find her! Why are we just standing here, we should—"

"Soomin was in Houston," Jasper cuts in, crisp and with a warning finality.

I drag in a deep, bleak breath.

Before the silence can stretch again, Jayk walks over to the truck beside mine. He flips the trunk and leans in.

"I've got two rifles, three pistols. Ammo. A fuck-ton, give or take. Some frags, C4—bitch me out later, Dom, we're going to need it—bug out bag, a few cases of bottled water. Camping gear." He scowls. "That's for one. I'm not sharing."

So many things, and none of it matters. We're too late. We're outmatched. Outplayed.

And my family is dead.

They don't need me.

Jasper is staring in pale bemusement at Jayk, but Dom just nods. "Good. Pass them around. Thomas?"

Thomas lifts a tatted shoulder. "Just a rifle. One pistol. Bug out bag. That's it, sorry, Cap."

"Fine. Lucky?" Dom ducks into the truck to get my pistol out of the glove compartment.

Apples assault me, and I shiver.

Jayk pulls two rifles out of his truck locker, and Lucky looks between him and Dom, his eyes big and wide. "What *about* me? I didn't bring anything!"

Jayk, Dom, and Thomas exchange a look, nonplussed.

Lucky backs up defensively, jostling me, but I barely notice. Two more cars rip out of the lot.

Off to go find their own people's ash clouds.

Lucky points at Dom. "Oh, no way. *I* am not the problem here. I was coming here to get laid. Who the hell brings an arsenal to a *kink club*?" He looks between them, *tsk*ing. "You guys have problems. Way too paranoid. Jasper, write that down."

Standing stiffly to one side, rubbing his forehead, Jasper gives him a flat look. His hair's a mess, and his blacksnake is uncoiled by his side, the delicate fall dragging limply in the gravel. Jasper doesn't seem to care that it's snagging.

Strange.

"Things have been going to shit for years," Jayk sneers at Lucky. He tosses me a rifle, and my hands come up to catch it before I even register the throw. "You're fucking stupid not to prepare."

The rifle bites my palms.

Hard. Cold.

Real.

"Yeah, Jayky boy's right on this one. They might not have *said* we were on red alert, but as if it wasn't obvious. You didn't think you might want to protect your ass, just in case?" Thomas laughs, giving Lucky a good-natured shove. His hands are shaking, but no one says anything. "Or were you just counting on me to protect you?"

Lucky snorts, shoving him back. "Hey, I *was* prepared." He tugs a foil packet out of his back pocket, then holds it in between two fingers. "My ass was protected all night long, baby."

He flicks the condom at Jayk. His snicker cuts off a second later when a tossed rifle hits him hard in the chest.

Thomas laughs again, and it's too damn loud, like he's trying to eat up all the strangeness in the air with the sound.

I drag in another slow breath, disoriented. They're just out of step, and the uncanniness sends prickles up my spine. They're marionettes, not quite lifelike, and they're still standing there, acting like this is normal. Like it's a normal call out. Normal orders.

Don't they see how strange that is?

Thomas walks over to his car, still grinning. Laughing off-key, Lucky flips off Jayk.

And someone screams like God just ripped their soul to shreds.

Every hair on the back of my neck stands on end.

Things aren't *normal* right now.

They aren't normal right now.

The last star winks out, and I turn my rifle over in my hands.

Dom tries to catch my eye, smiling slightly, like he wants to pretend, too . . . but as soon as our eyes meet, he flinches. Just for a moment, I see the panic snake through him, but he chokes it out. His face closes down, and he turns, tucking my pistol into his belt. Thankfully, he shuts the car door again.

Then he's moving. Barking orders to civilians. Snapping them into motion. *Normal.*

Almost.

I don't bother to help. There's no point, not this time. It's not like a few extra weapons or a few extra orders will make any difference when whole cities are gone. Bases. All our meaningful intelligence and decision makers.

It's Code Alpha.

We're fucked six ways from Sunday no matter what we do.

God. Half a day. That's all it was. I was off with the faeries for half a day, and my world disappeared.

Lucky kicks back against the truck beside me. He still smells like sex, but it doesn't matter. Why should anything matter anymore?

"Okay, but seriously, how am I the only one who wasn't packing?" he complains. "This doesn't feel right. I'm clearing out the base when we get there; this can't happen again. My arsenal is going to be *way* bigger than Jayk's."

Rolling his eyes, Jayk slams a magazine into Lucky's hands, then heads back to his truck. Dom is still shouting, rounding people up, and the wind slices at us.

Lucky hands me a magazine, and after a moment, I take it.

My rifle is familiar. In a fast, snapping moment, I have it loaded, deadly cold and charged. Muscle memory. Real, beyond shock or strangeness. They made killing an instinct.

I wonder how many people I've killed now.

I wonder if it's more than I've saved.

I was a good, God-fearing man, once. Church every Sunday,

and I minded my cussing. But in the end, I sold my soul for this gun. I sold it to my country to protect my family. But I should have known better.

I should have been drinking punch and making fat, happy babies.

Tears burn hot in the back of my throat, turning the world misty and silver again. *God, help me*. I should have been with them. This whole time, I should have been with them.

I should have died with them.

"They hit LA," Lucky says suddenly.

My lips part over a soft, wet breath.

Why couldn't I have just died with them?

"It's fine, though. Don't worry," he assures me. His eyes are searching, but they're not seeing. "My folks . . . they weren't there. I'm sure of it."

The cremated sky doesn't move anymore. It's silent. Blurry. God isn't helping me or anyone today. Maybe they've had enough of all of us.

I know I have.

Another tear slips over my nose, and I sniff it back, but too many follow. I can't see anymore, but it doesn't matter. My rifle is loaded, hard and heavy, and it feels like it should. I can check it blind.

Lucky glances over at me, and his eyes burn the side of my face.

"You . . . you agree, right?" he finally whispers. "That they made it out?"

My hands pause on the safety, and what he's saying breaks through my foggy brain. My eyes sink shut. There's a dullness deep in my chest, and it's spreading through my insides.

He doesn't want me to answer that.

When I don't reply, he looks away again, and I hear him swallow. "I think they made it. They're okay. It's going to be okay."

Is there even a point to living in a world when our families are gone?

When *family* is gone?

Lucky presses his shoulder against mine, and he leans into me. His voice is soft when he says, "Maybe . . . maybe your folks made it out, too. I mean, you did. It's possible, right?"

It's too much.

My heart is dying.

I walk away, not even sure where I'm going. I'm not sure there's anywhere *to* go anymore. It's all swirling around me. The world is disappearing.

My gun is so, so cold.

Certain.

I stop, looking down at it as I cry.

I can almost see all the blood spilling over my hands. All the red tears God wept over me and my choices.

"Give me the gun, Beaumont." Jasper's voice is careful, but it comes from so far away. It's almost lost in the swirl.

The gun bites into my palms. "It's not right, Jasper. None of this is right."

"Of course it isn't."

"How are they all doing that?" I sob. "Dom just ordering people around. They're making *jokes*. It's all pretend. They're playing pretend."

"It's how they cope. There's no normal way to behave right now. Please give me the gun, Beaumont."

He's swirling away.

Or maybe I am.

"It's done. We failed. They're all dead, and we're all ghosts. You just don't see it yet. The world disappeared. We can't get it back."

I can't see anything, but the gun is in my hands. It's such a familiar weight. I loaded it so carefully, with more bullets that are only taking me further from my family. I'm already damned. In this life or the next, I'm never going to see them again.

Jasper's loafers crunch. "The others understand what's happened, but there are still people here. People they can help. They're doing what they can. We're not all dead. Not yet."

I look down the barrel of the rifle. It's dark and strange inside. "We're going to disappear too."

"*Give me the gun, Beaumont.*"

My hands shake, that heat scalding the back of my throat. My finger finds metal, and I sob. "I want to go home, Jasper. Please, I just want to go home."

Jasper turns sharply, shouting like a whipcrack. "Dominic!"

Hot tears slip over my cheeks.

His hand bites into my shoulder, cold and firm. It slows the swirl enough to see his dark, steady eyes. They're stained wet too.

But they're as certain as my gun.

"I know this feels impossible, and that your whole world is crumbling," he says in a low, urgent voice, "but, Beaumont, it's only so because you love so very, very deeply. It's an exceptional thing. What you feel for your family is agonizing and it is *beautiful*. And very soon, there are going to be far too many people who need your medicine, and your care . . . and who will be in desperate need of a heart like yours in this world."

Dom appears behind Jasper, corpse pale, his pupils blown

wide in fear, and my heart splinters apart on sight. I break, weeping, shaking from head to toe.

Slowly, gently, Jasper pulls the rifle from my grip.

I let him take it.

His breath is shaky, but his hand stays steady on my shoulder, and he squeezes hard.

"You're not a ghost, my dear friend. None of us are. Ghosts don't hurt like this. That is a uniquely human misery."

I can't breathe. I can't *breathe* without them.

"You son of a bitch," Dom shouts, storming up on me.

He grabs me, I think. I don't care. I sob into his shoulder.

"You son of a bitch," he repeats, shaking as hard as me. "You stupid son of a bitch!"

"I'm sorry. I'm sorry," I choke out between floods of tears.

"*Are* you?"

I turn into his neck. "My whole family. They're all . . . Dom, they're all—"

Dom grips the back of my hair painfully, holding me fiercely. "*I'm* your family. Beau, I'm your family. You don't get to go anywhere, because *I need you*, okay?"

The world is *done*.

But his tears are splashing me, too. Burning. Real. Dom is real.

"No, I can't. Please don't. Don't you put that on me." I try to catch my breath, but it's too far gone. "Please don't put that on me."

Dom's voice lowers, breaking. "You're my brother. You're the only real family I ever had. You're the *only one* I can't lose. I need you. I need you for this. I can't do it alone. I know you lost everything today, but you still have me. You always have me."

I cry into him, holding on to him like a lifeline.

There's no gun. No pie. No world.

Only Dom.

Until there's not.

"Give them a moment, all of you. They need space."

A shaky voice replies, "Was he really going to—"

"Just shut up, Lucky," Jayk mutters, and strangely, he's even shakier. "All of this is fucked."

How am I meant to do this? I don't know how to do this.

I only realize I've whispered it when Dom growls, "We do our jobs. There are other civilians, other moms and kids, and they're going to be scared out of their mind. They need us. We need to protect them."

I pull back, shaking my head. "I can't do it. How can I be strong for these people, Dom? I can't—"

Dom hits my shoulder, hard, cutting me off. "Yes, you can. You can take it. I can take it. We can because we have to." His eyes blaze. "Someone has to carry the load, Beau. That's what a soldier does. We carry that fucking load so they don't have to." He grips my shirt, and his jaw works. "And when you can't carry it, I'll carry you, too."

I squeeze a hand over my eyes, swallowing down my tears. "That's your dad talking. And he's going to get you killed."

Dom lets me go. "The Colonel is a stronger man than I'll ever be—and we'll all be grateful for it in the end. He might be the only one who can fix this."

Fix this.

It's so bitter, the worst pretending yet, that I almost want to laugh.

He wants to carry me, all of my grief for me, all of everyone's, and he still doesn't see it.

There's no fixing this.

But he still wants to try.

I look around. Jasper. Jayk. Lucky. Thomas. They're all here, looped around us, cutting us off from the civilians, giving us privacy.

Protecting us.

In an instant, I see more than peaches and pie.

I see Thomas dragging me back under cover right before a frag went off. Lucky catcalling me as I skidded over sand dunes. Jayk's bullets blistering my eardrums as he kept the enemy off me so I could get to our guys. Jasper handing me a tissue as I broke down after Nick died.

I was wrong to call them co-workers.

They're so much more than that.

"It's not the family you want, Beau," Dom says gruffly, "but it's the one we have."

Dom.

He's standing tall, somehow. Still. Even after this, he's ready to take it all on.

The clouds shift. A soft, bare break in the deadened mass. Six bright, impossible stars wink down.

Six. It's always been my favorite number.

The number of freckles on my ass.

The number of shots it takes me to pass out.

The number of people in my family.

Old. And new.

I look back down at Dom, at the fear that's eating at his foundations.

When he finally crumbles under all that pressure he's putting on himself, he'll need someone to carry him for a change. Someone to put him back on his feet.

A family.

Slowly, I straighten, walking back over to him.

I'm not making the same mistake again. I'm going to be there for my family. To keep them safe. To live with them . . . or to die with them. But we're not going to be apart. Not anymore.

I look around at the others, and one by one, their shoulders relax.

I clasp Dom's wrist.

"Then let's see these people safe."

Episode Four

Lucky

Lucky, ride with Jasper. We're consolidating vehicles," Dom orders distractedly.

I wave him off, shifting around to keep Beau in view as he finishes up with the med supplies. My heart is still pounding, and I can't make it stop.

Too close, too close, too goddamned close.

Guiltily, I grip my cell. I know it's bad to even think it, when Beau's still moving like every breath hurts . . . but I'm glad my folks are safe.

Now I just need everyone to stay that way.

We can figure all this out, I know it. We just need to stay together.

Beau quickly takes his final inventory, then packs away the rest of the medical supplies into his bag. When he looks up, I hurriedly push off his truck, shoving my sweaty, shaking hands in my pockets. Casual.

You know, like I wasn't just watching him like an anxious mother duck.

And I'm not the only one.

Thomas has been sitting next to Beau for five minutes, nonchalantly sharpening the hunting knife Jayk gave him . . . sharpening it like Jayk doesn't always keep his blades primed and ready for a good stabbing.

Jayk has aerials covered. He's up in the back of his truck, retying the same tarp over his supplies for the third time, sneaking worried scowls down at the doc.

And Dom isn't even trying to hide how he's hovering.

He might be shouting orders, but he hasn't taken his eye off Beau.

The kinksters are scurrying around, stripping the club of supplies and finishing loading up their cars. We should probably help them. There are more than a few people as bad or worse than Beau right now, but the guys don't seem willing to let him out of their sight—and neither am I.

No matter how hard it is to watch him like this. All dull and sad and grief lost.

I mean . . . it's definitely not as hard as watching him stare down a gun barrel like he's about to deep-throat death.

Still not great, though.

Beau's gaze swings from me to Jayk, to Dom, to Thomas . . . and he blows out a low, irritated breath.

He gets up, slinging the medical bag over his shoulder. "Can we beat feet already?"

The concerned line between Dom's eyes deepens. "Two minutes." He flicks his gaze to me. "You. With Jasper. Bring up the rear."

I blink away from my anxious Beau-watch, Dom's orders finally registering.

Ride.

In a car.

With *Jasper*.

In the *rear*.

Ooh, yeah. That's not a good idea.

Clearing my throat, I offer Dom a shaky, winning smile. "So about that, I'm gonna have to pass." I toss a thumb over my shoulder at my baby, sleek and tight and gotta-go red. Zero to sixty in two point nine seconds. She's polished up and gleaming under the harsh fluorescents like she's blowing me kisses. I shrug. "Can't leave my girl behind, you know? And she isn't into three-ways."

The immediate visual of Jasper, me, and that bike is filthy enough to make me pray for myself. For the sake of my immortal soul or whatever, I really need to stay away from him.

Okay.

I mean.

Not *away* away.

Just somewhere outside touching distance. Like back in his therapist chair—the one that looks too much like a casting couch. It's far enough for me not to do something stupid, but close enough that I can still watch the shape of his mouth when he talks.

At some point, he became my favorite form of masochism.

As if summoned by the thought, Jasper walks over to Beau, handing him a first aid kit and murmuring something under his breath. He's sleek and stupidly hot in all black. His shirt is open by more buttons than is good for my health, and the blacksnake coiled at his hip is enough to whip every fantasy I have into action.

His demonstration tonight was a real problem for me.

The masochist he worked over, Katie, was a weeping, shaking mess by the time he was done. Every stroke was vicious. Every welt he left was glowing and elegant. When he was done, Katie's domme collected her for aftercare with an awe I felt in my bones.

No one was taking care of *me*, though.

In the crowd, I was just as messy—and I've got to say, the customer service on these shows sucks. No aftercare at all for the slutty, secret voyeur left shaking behind a gibbet cage, trying not to be seen.

Well, not unless you count watching Jasper drain his icy water in one long suck. Or how he patted the sweat from his forehead with the prettiest handkerchief I've ever seen. Or romantically rubbing myself out to the image of him in the toilet stalls.

Can't say I felt a whole lot better about myself after that one, though.

I need to scrub the whole thing from my brain. I should replace it with something wholesome for a change. Maybe something sobering.

Like his wedding ring.

Or, you know, the world currently burning down around us. That's a boner-killer for sure.

Slinging my new rifle back over my shoulder, I clear my throat and look back at Dom. "Yep. Definitely taking the Ducati."

"Damn it, Lucky, no. Your bike is dangerous, and it chugs gas like a frat boy. We conserve fuel. Ride with Jasper," Dom says impatiently, and he's forgotten about me before he's finished talking. He narrows his eyes on Phill across the lot, where he's furtively tucking a pistol into the front of his jeans.

"For fuck's sake." Dom's voice lifts into a shout as he walks off. "Take that gun out of your pants, asshole, you're going to shoot your dick off."

Jasper pauses beside Beau, his cool gaze flicking between me and Dom.

Thomas gets up off the ground, snorting as he sheaths the knife. "You just got voluntold, baby boy." He claps me on the shoulder as he passes me. "But hey, maybe you'll get a free session out of it." Eyes twinkling, his voice lowers. "Not the kind you want, though, I bet."

"Hey, you're funny," I say, and he grins—then ducks away before I can slug him.

He turns as he backs away. "At least Douglas owns deodorant. I've been enlisted into King's musty crapbox for the next four hours."

Jayk jumps down from the bed of his truck, scowling at Thomas. "You don't shut up, I'm tying you to the back instead. We can see how good you run to base."

Thomas rolls his eyes, but he climbs into the passenger side of Jayk's truck, sparing one final, sobered look at Beau.

Beau seems to catch it.

His own truck door slams pointedly, and I flinch a little.

It must be terrible, knowing everyone you love is dead.

Damn it. It's so hard to face him like this. He's too raw. Too real. It happens sometimes out on an op, when things go south and nothing's looking up. Most guys in a group like that, they joke and bullshit each other. You have to keep it light, because fear is infectious . . . and scared people do dangerous things.

Still, it happens. When things get bad enough, people are

always going to crack. You've just got to make sure you've got a team around who'll help you glue up the fractures.

Trying to glue myself together first, I head over to Beau's door—but as I brush past Jasper, he touches my elbow.

"Dominic told you to ride with me?" he asks, silken and unreadable.

His fingers sink fire into my blood.

Yeah, so this is *so* not outside touching distance.

"Ah— Yeah. I just need to grab my bag," I tell him, my heart jumping in riotous, jittery ways. I meet his dark, intent eyes for half a second, then look back at Beau, sitting in his truck and staring at nothing. "Just . . . give me two seconds, okay?"

Adjusting my rifle strap over my shoulder, I knock on his window without waiting for a reply from Jasper.

Beau's jaw flexes, but he finally winds it down so I can lean inside. It smells like cinnamon and apple pie, and my stomach pangs.

Beau's mama made the best pies.

"What, Lucky?" he asks tiredly, and I work up a grin for him.

He needs it.

Just gotta do my thing. Keep it casual. Friendly. *Light.*

"Hey buddy!" I drop an easy shrug, checking my nails. "Not doing much. Just popping in, you know. Killing time." Nope. Not that. "I mean, spending time. Alive. Being alive. Waiting?"

Be the glue.

Beau blinks, then turns to me, very slowly, and I awkwardly rub the back of my neck.

But I can't help but laugh.

"I'm just saying hi!" I drum on the door. "Aaand maybe

checking for sharp objects." His brow crinkles incredulously as I really do sneak in a scan of the cabin. "Coiled rope . . . Season Eight of *Game of Thrones* . . ."

His brow crinkles. "Are you joking . . . about suicide?"

Oh. Right.

Be lighter than that.

"Too soon?"

He stares at me and I wince. Yeah. Too soon.

I scramble to think of something less bleak, but all I've got are some dusty knock-knock jokes and one about a priest that might be even worse.

Damn . . . I'm shitty glue.

He rubs a hand over his jaw, and I see the moment he breaks. A wild, disbelieving snort escapes him. "You're really fucked up, you know that?"

"Dude, I wasn't the one bobbing for bullets!" I run a hand through my hair, caught somewhere between panic and relief.

He's here again. Maybe just for now, but . . . he's here.

"Bobbing for—" Beau chokes on a horrified laugh. He shoves me out of the window, then leans out of it to gesture at Jasper. "Would you get this asshole some sensitivity training on the way to base? I reckon he's missed a session or twelve."

"I'm retired," Jasper says, and a hint of wry deprecation slips into his voice. "And I'm not sure anyone could teach this submissive reverence."

It runs illicitly close to my earlier thoughts, watching him with his whip.

I roll my shoulders nervously. "Switch," I correct him, though it sounds weak even to me. "You couldn't teach this . . . this *switch* reverence."

One impossibly dark brow lifts.

He doesn't even speak, just lifts that one knowing, pitying brow, and I die a thousand deaths.

He *knows*.

How willingly I'd crawl to him. The way I'd let him flay me to the bone for a smile. I don't even have to say it. With that one arrogant eyebrow, I'm sure of it.

He *knows*.

A slight curve touches his grim lips. "Go get your things, Lucien."

I . . . am in so much trouble.

Beau slowly looks between us, then pointedly ducks back into his truck. I linger, my hand on the window frame like a lifeline. I look at Beau, panicked.

He gives me half a smile, not quite meeting my eyes. "I'm okay, Lucky. Go on now."

He's okay? Jasper *knows*.

Which, okay, objectively speaking, isn't as bad as his stuff.

Better reel that one in.

Sobering a little, I watch his face, like I might be able to see the cracks in him just by looking. "Are you? Are you really?"

Beau tenses. "I'm here for these people. I'm here for you." His face firms, and he finally meets my eyes.

I immediately wish he didn't.

Finally, he adds softly, "We're dealing with the same thing, after all."

I frown. It takes a second to realize what he means.

My parents.

A different kind of panic ices my veins. "Oh no. No, I mean. They weren't there. They're fine. Somewhere between LA and Vegas, probably. Not that— I'm sorry it happened to you, though. No one should have to live through that."

My pulse flutters recklessly at my throat, even though I know it's fine.

Beau gives me a long, measured look, sadness touching his eyes. "No. They shouldn't."

The grief in him churns my stomach, and I back away.

Fast.

My foot hits a rock, and I stumble. When I reach out to right myself, Jasper grips my forearm, holding me steady. His dark, dark eyes are still on my face.

There's an edginess in me when I stand up, and I can't quite bring myself to stop gripping his arm. But he doesn't move. Only his hair lifts in the low, restless breeze. A whisper around his face.

"Let's head out!" Dom shouts, stalking up to Beau's truck and letting himself into the driver's side.

Forcing a deep breath, I let Jasper go, then stride over to my bike. I don't look at him again. I don't leave much with my girl, so it's a quick trip.

I brush my hand over her with a quick, surprisingly fierce burst of regret.

Dom's right. She doesn't make sense for a job like this. She was built for highways and playtime, not road blockades and a potential land war. But she was my first big purchase after I moved out. One of my best friends between deployments.

It doesn't feel right to lose her, too.

Slowly, an ugly Volvo pulls in beside me. I *think* it's meant to be silver, but I've seen dirty dishwater that gets me harder.

Jasper's sitting in the driver's seat.

"Okay, no," I say, disgusted.

Jasper eyes my bike, then me. His eyes lift up. "Just get in the car, Lucien."

Getting to my feet, I double-check my rifle and my maga-zines are secure, then pocket my baby's key. "*That* is not a car. That's a cry for help."

"It isn't like I'm out street racing for loose drugs." His fingers tap impatiently on the steering wheel at a perfect ten and two. "It's a respectable car."

I start circling the wheeled yawn and shake my head. "Nope. You're just heading out for some groceries. Maybe you can take your grandmother to bingo on the way back."

Tentatively, I try to open the car door, only to realize it's locked.

You have to be . . .

Through the glass, I give Jasper a long, pitying look. He might know I'm a slut for him, but now *I* know he's a boring old prude.

Pursing his lips, Jasper unlocks the door, and I slide in—hesitating only slightly when I see the back seat piled high with neatly packed suitcases and two expensive-looking artworks. I rest my rifle between my legs.

Jasper looks over his shoulder, adjusting his mirrors, and I shove my tongue into my cheek at the slow, fastidious care. He gives me a slicing, sideways look.

"Safety and reliability are admirable qualities," he says silk-ily, pulling out. Low, cool jazz begins to play from the speakers, and I shake my head.

"No, no, it's great. I can't wait to ride ten miles under the speed limit." I drop my seat back and stretch out. "I need a nap."

Ahead of us, Beau's truck disappears into the trees, heading out toward base. Car after car leaves after them. Jayk and Thomas in Jayk's monster wheeler sit somewhere in the middle, then finally, there's just us and a dozen empty cars sitting in the lot like gravestones.

Then Jasper drives away from Darkside too.

An edginess starts to creep in as I watch my Ducati wink out of the rearview mirror. The usual battle jitters, only this time we don't have a full briefing and a plan. This time, we have an emergency broadcast and a single phone message.

Unable to stop myself, I check my phone again, but I only see the same messages from my parents sitting there from yesterday. I tap out another text and send it, even though I can see there's no signal.

Message failed to deliver

I swallow. Maybe it will go through when everything's back up.

Shoving my phone away again, I glance at Jasper. His eyes are on the road, focused and calm, but there's a grim set to his mouth that makes me think he didn't miss a thing.

The long, barren streets stretch on and on ahead of us, our convoy of cars the only thing breaking the eerie stillness. Darkside is tucked out of the way—the only people who show up are people arriving for a reason. It'll be twenty minutes before we even hit a town. An hour or more before we get close to base.

Jasper's car smells like rich leather and sharp cleaning products, and he maneuvers it with easy confidence. He's so close like this. Close enough to breathe in. Close enough to touch. Between the wicked glimpses of his chest and slight flex of his thighs, I'm almost convinced that the Volvo *is* sexy.

Thirty miles an hour with Jasper isn't slow enough.

Reaching down, Jasper unhitches the blacksnake from his

hip and hands it to me. "Put this away? The bag is in the glove compartment."

The cruel leather slips through my palms, and my pulse skyrockets.

"Say please," I tsk.

I don't even sound breathless. Nailed it.

His quick, arch look makes me smirk, and I raise my brows expectantly. The challenge of it thrills through me. We don't talk like this, not ever. It's always been him on his couch and me on mine, outside a few brief, stilted interactions at social events.

How does the sadist handle being scolded?

Jasper scans my face for a cool moment before he turns back to the road, still calm. Still responsible.

Disappointment takes the air out of some of my excitement.

Then, without taking his eyes from the road, he leans over slowly, right into my personal space, opening the glove compartment. My breath stalls in my chest. He's burning hot, just inches away. His lashes are a secret veil and there's a malicious divot in his top lip that I *need* to suck.

Jasper pulls out a black satin bag.

He tilts his head toward me, just slightly. Confidingly. "Stop being a brat, Lucien, and do as you're told."

He drops the bag on my lap—so neatly over my fucking erection that a startled, humiliated blush scalds my cheeks—and his eyes flash to mine.

They're the deep, impossible brown of long-buried oak.

And they're full of quiet mockery.

"*Please*," he murmurs, with pointed, devastating politeness.

He withdraws back into his seat, and my breath shudders out of me in a shaky laugh.

Okay then.

Sadist, one.

Lucky, really fucking close to a big "O."

Jasper turns a casual corner, totally composed. Swallowing, I lift the bag with one hand, holding on to the whip with the other.

"Keep it in a loose coil, don't bend it. I'll hang it when . . ." He frowns, his lips pursing briefly. "When I can, I suppose."

My body is still tingling, so I decide to let that one go. None of us knows where we'll be even in the next few hours.

"I know what to do with a whip, Jasper," I manage to tease as I check the coils, then slip it into the bag.

He tenses, then gives me a long, searching look. When he turns back to the road, his hands grip tighter on the steering wheel.

"Indeed."

I should leave it there. I know I should. But seeing him like this is delicious. Too rare and fascinating to stop. He's not running through debriefs of ops, or reproaching me for making light of the rank bump I didn't get for "not acting in a manner appropriate for the commission of duty"—which we both knew was code for being too flippant.

"It matters to you, Lucien," Jasper scolded me after I spent fifteen minutes complaining about it, so much more bothered than I should have been.

"Well, sure. It'd be nice. I don't know why they care if I'm not scowling enough, though. I can do the job. I just don't need to act like the weight of the world is crushing me to do it."

"You're doing it again, right now. This coping mechanism is a problem."

"It's not a—"

"Lucien, what is the harm in showing how much you care? Do

you feel it will hurt more when you're disappointed? If every-
thing's a joke, then at least you're in on it—is that it?" Those dark,
serious eyes. "For someone so willing to play the fool, you're so
afraid to truly feel like one. But being serious about something,
wanting *something and going after it . . . that isn't foolish,*
Lucien. It's not embarrassing, win or lose. It's brave."

I don't know why I'm thinking about that—and thinking
about it *now*.

My psychologist would never dream of being flippant. Wise,
ancient, knowing. He was born pensive and thoughtful. He's
forever serious.

Except for when he's on stage, whipping subbies into bliss.

Except for right now.

Why *is* he playing with me now? Is this a game I even want
to play? It's one thing to watch him. To joke with him. Even to
wake up with cum on my thighs and his eyes in my head. It's a
whole other thing to be within touching distance of him,
married him. I can't be serious about Jasper. I just can't.

This is a game I can only lose.

"You probably shouldn't call me a brat," I say quietly. "It's
unprofessional."

His face darkens.

"I'm retired. I'm not your therapist any longer," he reminds
me tightly. Then he shoots me an edged look. "And I know a
brat when I see one, Lucien."

Oh shit.

I tear my gaze away from him, strangely panicked. No, not
strangely. I know why. This is dangerous—and in a way that
could really end up hurting me. Because when he says things
like that, like *retired*, it feels like something's getting stripped
away. Like the walls between us are being pulled down, brick by

brick, and I need every single brick to stay intact so I don't do something stupid.

Towns start to slowly unwind past us as we near civilization. The roads are junked up with people frantically packing, and cars heading to the same place. Everyone needs to get to base.

But as much as I know I should be thinking about *that*, about dying worlds and dying people. I just can't. It's not a real problem yet. There's nothing I can do.

And Jasper's right here, tugging at all my thoughts.

Damn it, why *did* he retire?

He's thirty-eight. I know he has family money, but everyone knows he's one of the best in his field. He worked for this, and he's so damn *good* at it.

And why is he *moving*?

This car is loaded up. He wasn't going for a weekend, or even a few weeks.

He's leaving town.

I heard him and Soomin talking about Bristlebrook before, once, at a fundraiser for injured vets. Some old lodge out in the middle of nowhere they visit in the summers. Probably full of ancient, musty sheets and dust mites.

It doesn't make sense.

Jasper is an indoor cat, anyone can see that. What the hell is he running from?

And why does it have to be so far away from *me*?

The stupid Volvo is suddenly too small. I need my bike and open, *solitary* air all around me. I can't be closed in here with him, not with blacksnakes that could lay me open. Not with his pitiless hands tugging at the wheel. Not with him retiring and moving away and stirring up all this panic I shouldn't have.

Not with him calling me *brat*.

But it's not like we can stop. Despite how unsafe I'm suddenly feeling, we're in a convoy of civilians who need to get to safety. I just need to calm down. This flirting is getting out of hand. I need . . .

My gaze darts to his left hand, searching for his wedding ring.

That ring always breaks me. Soothes me. It's his brand. His collar. The thing that always saves me from myself. Because he's *not mine*. He belongs to Soomin. Lovely, elegant Soomin with her thriving corporate events business and perfect sense of style.

I've talked to her exactly twice, and that was enough to know that she's a good person who cares about him a whole lot.

And maybe, privately, I can still wonder whether they really are a perfect fit, when they always have a foot of space between them whenever they're together. When their smiles for each other are polite and affectionate, but in a way that I might smile at an old friend I hadn't seen in a while. Maybe I can wonder.

But that's it.

I don't know them. Not really. Every single relationship I've ever seen is so different from the next one. I sure as hell can't know what they're like when doors are closed. He chose her. That's all that matters.

So, I just need to see the ring—just a teensy, tiny, cuff-like reminder that I am *completely* fucking delusional—and I'll be able to pull my shit together.

Probably.

Hopefully.

Only when I look . . . it's not there.

Jasper's long, slender fingers are white-knuckled over the steering wheel—and all of them are stripped naked.

I sit forward, rattled.

He *needs* that ring.

"Jasper, your ring," I say before I can stop myself. "You didn't leave it at the club, did you?"

Maybe he doesn't wear it during a scene. Whips can rub on rings, I've seen it before.

Except . . . Jasper is right-handed.

Jasper's jaw flexes.

"Don't worry about it," he says, clipped.

Don't *worry*?

"No, really, we should go back. You can't lose that," I stammer, shocked.

How can he just dismiss that? It's his *wedding ring*. He can't just forget about it, not now.

Oh, God. Horror creeps into me, filling me with black, guilty little bites as I remember our conversation earlier. After everything with Beau, I wasn't thinking, but . . . Soomin.

He really can't lose his ring now.

Not if she's . . . dead.

"Lucien, I mean it. Leave it alone," Jasper says, with such chilly, lethal warning that I flinch back into my seat.

The satin sheen of his shirt makes his skin glow, turning him otherworldly. But his face is forbidding—all sharp cheekbones and a mouth set harshly enough to cut.

Of course he doesn't want to talk about it.

Guilt swamps me. What the fuck is wrong with me? Here I am checking him out, flirting, when his wife just died. She died *hours* ago.

I stare at his profile, seeing his composure differently now. He's studied it, I'm sure of it. How to stay cool and expressionless, how not to react. Beau is an open wound of pain and grief, Thomas is cracking jokes and fretting, Jayk is basically giving out free hugs compared to how he usually is, and even Dom was splintering over Beau.

But Jasper has it together.

He caught Beau. Helped Dom. He was there, stepping up. Always, in the background, he's working us through our shit.

My jokes mean jack shit.

Jasper is the glue.

No matter what he has going on himself, he makes sure we're sticking together.

I see his throat work as he swallows hard, his entire body strung tight. On him, grief is silent. Deep and internal. And in the deep night, lit only by the red glow of taillights ahead of us, his pain is beautiful.

My heart stumbles in my chest. God, he haunts me.

Every night when I go to bed. Every spare minute when my thoughts slip away. I need to make it stop. This can't work. Those bricks are still there, right? The wall between us? He's my . . . okay. Okay, well. He's not my psychologist. He's right about that—retired and all. So that's one brick gone.

But he *is* married.

Or . . . I mean. I look over at his hand, lingering on his bare ring finger.

He *was* married.

If Soomin is dead, that kind of makes him single now, right?

As soon as the nightmarishly fucked-up thought hits me, I rub both hands over my face, cringing back into my—admittedly comfortable—seat.

Jesus fuck, Lucky. Even for you, that's bad.

"Lucien?" Jasper asks sharply.

Yeah. Like I'm voicing *that* one— *"Hey Jaz, pretty great your wife died, huh? Wanna cuddle and stuff?"*

"Nope. We're good. Just going to hell. Can't wait. Should be toasty," I groan.

"I didn't know you were religious."

"I think I need to start," I mutter.

He gives me a curious look that I'm too ashamed to acknowledge. He might have something to his sessions. Maybe I do use flippancy as a coping mechanism.

But everyone needs to cope, right? Surely there are worse ways.

Just ask Beau.

Yep. Definitely straight to hell.

Okay, okay. So, it's a problem. But how is anyone meant to deal with all of this? I look outside, at the roiling, ashy sky and the cars screaming past in the opposite direction. Flash after flash of terrified faces.

How do you even begin to think about what this could mean?

"We're almost there," Jasper murmurs, and I realize I've been staring out the window for too long.

So much of the world looks exactly the same as it did seven hours ago when I drove in here. Only the people look different.

And that sky.

My skin starts to itch, and I tug out my phone again, staring at the messages I've already memorized.

> MOMMIKINS: You're BACK?! You get your ass over here NOW, baby! I miss that gorgeous face

> POPSICLE: Ur mom is dranK

> POPSICLE: dAnk

POPSICLE: DRUNK

POPSICLE: Phone sux. Wnt to call?

MOMMIKINS: HE'S drunk I'M fine.

MOMMIKINS: NO! WAIT! don't come here! let's do vegas! cha-CHING!

MOMMIKINS: i want to see someone pop a ping pong out of their hoo-ha!

POPSICLE: I only had 2 dinks

POPSICLE: DRINKS

MOMMIKINS sent video

MOMMIKINS: i could do that. U think they do classes?

POPSICLE: dnt watch that

POPSICLE: jesus

POPSICLE: i need another dink

ME: Wait! For real this time? I could get down with vegas. Sign me up!

ME: And stop crushing mom's dreams, papa bear - she can ping any pong she wants to

MOMMIKINS: thx, sweetie

POPSICLE: u get to take her to classes then

MOMMIKINS: vegaasssssss! road tripppp! let's go tonight!!

And then yesterday:

> ME: So I'm assuming you guys are mainlining water and Tylenol this morning— you want me to book the hotel?

> MOMMIKINS: book what?

> POPSICLE: tlk soon. Head hrts

I stare at those for a long minute before I scroll down. The last messages are from today. And they only go one way.

> ME: You guys left already, right?

> Message failed to deliver

> Call failed

> ME: Drive to me. I'll be at base. Just keep going, don't stop for anything but gas.

> Message failed to deliver

It's fine.

They didn't need me to book anything, because they already took off. My parents are reckless. Impulsive. They might not have traveled much, but they're adventurers at heart. Knowing them, they probably hitchhiked half the way then got distracted by a glassblowers' convention in the middle of the desert. Every time I talk to them, they have a new story.

This . . . this is just going to be a good one.

They're fine.

Jasper is eyeing me, his gaze flicking between my phone and

my face, when the convoy starts to slow. Not-too-distant pops of blistering noise puncture the air in short bursts.

Gunfire.

Someone's shooting. More pops go off, faster and faster, and adrenaline-hot anticipation begins to fill my stomach.

All right, then. Maybe several someones.

I grab my rifle.

Jasper pulls the car to a halt, and I shove open the car door. In front of us, the town of Franklin is on fire, the sloping road blockaded by an abandoned car and a fallen utility pole that sparks with live wires.

And in the town center, there's a vicious firefight in front of a massive pharmacy.

I squint, but from down here, I can't get a good angle. Moving fast, I climb up onto the hood of the Volvo, staring down at the town.

"Get back inside your fucking cars until I say so. Now!" Dom snaps, storming up the line of the convoy as people start opening doors.

"Lucky, you got eyes?" Thomas calls from a few cars down as Jayk climbs up into the back of his truck to see for himself.

"Looks like civilians. Not seeing any greens." I scan the skies quickly, but it's hard to make out much through the thick, bruised cloud cover. "No eyes on the air. No obvious action, though."

"Roger that." Dom unslings his rifle, and I wince as a car horn starts shrieking in town. Pockets of fire blaze like will-o'-the-wisps.

This isn't right. We're only thirty miles from base, and Howards Evac Center is just on the other side of town, freshly built just ten years ago when things started heating up. There should be police, evac teams here working to get people to safety. Maybe even our guys, though I could see the Colonel wanting to keep boots on base.

But this town was meant to be safe.

It's not meant to be a war zone.

From the street, a woman lets out a bone-chilling scream and, at once, all Rangers' heads whip toward the fight. My pulse starts to pound.

Shit. Shit, shit, shit! I hate it when civs are involved.

A bloom of fire explodes from a supermarket window, and a half-dozen people burst out like a scattering herd.

And the screaming cuts off.

Suddenly, Beau breaks away from the head of the convoy, taking off at a run toward town. His medical bag is strapped to his back, and someone gave him his goddamned rifle.

"Dom! Beau!" Jayk snaps, and Dom wheels around, cursing when he spots Beau on the move.

"Thomas, you and Lucky protect the convoy," Dom shouts as he takes off after Beau. "Jayk, with me. Go!"

"Dom!" I jump down off the car, rifle in hand, ready to run after him. "I'm coming."

"Stay the fuck here, Lucky!"

He doesn't even look back. He's off, he and Jayk gaining ground on Beau.

Anxious fury ripping through me, I turn and kick the wheel of Jasper's car. "Fuck!"

Whirling back around, I run a hand into my hair, gripping it hard. With the way the road slopes, the curve of it, I can't see them from the ground. And I *need* to see.

I climb back up on Jasper's car, my boots scuffing up the awful paint job.

"Lucien, perhaps we should wait in the car," Jasper says carefully.

"Perhaps not," I mutter, scanning for the guys as they duck out of sight.

Thomas is doing the same thing on Jayk's truck.

As far as I can tell, there's two groups. One inside the pharmacy and one outside, both shooting at each other. There are at least two people caught in the street between them, huddling behind a few trash cans that won't stop shrapnel, let alone a bullet.

Shit.

"I think—"

Impatient, I glance down at him. "Jasper, I'm really not trying to be a dick, but you just don't know what you're talking about. I'm sorry about the boot marks, but I can't keep anyone safe from inside your car."

"I don't care about the car," Jasper mutters.

I look up just in time to see three bodies circling around the group outside the pharmacy, getting into position. They'll hit them with a pronged attack. I can't work out exactly how many they have to take down, but it won't be easy to do without lethal force.

Lethal force on civilians. Jesus Christ.

Over painkillers? Antibiotics?

A few inhalers?

But seriously, how has rioting started already? We're only hours into this thing. We're meant to have procedures for this, people on the ground to keep this shit from happening. How are we meant to organize a response if people are losing their damn minds?

One of the trash cans explodes in a surge of refuse, and

another blood-icing screech pierces the air. That's a hit. Someone was hit.

"Is everything okay?" one of the doms calls from his car.

"Does it *sound* okay, Phill?" a woman's voice snaps back, terrified.

"It's okay, folks, we've got this. Just stay down," Thomas calls out, strong and soothing. He's usually pretty good with this sort of thing. Usually, I am too. "If you have a firearm, keep the safety on but keep it on hand, okay?"

I rub my forehead, dancing up on my toes like I'll be able to see through the shadows any better. All the streetlights are out. Only angry red fires and the muzzle flashes of gunshots illuminate the night.

But I see one of the shooters' shadows go down, and hope springs up.

They've got this. The guys are on it. We'll fix it, get these people safe in the center and the town back in order. Maybe we'll need to drag some of the crew back from base to help, but we're together.

We can still fix it.

Some of the gunfire quietens a little, and my hand relaxes on my rifle.

It mostly just sucks that I'm on babysitting duty. I could use a good firefight to burn off some of this *stress*.

Eventually, I realize Jasper is leaning against the hood of his car, watching me.

I lift my brows at him in question, giving him an apologetic smile for snapping at him . . . even while I silently wonder how much trouble I'm in.

"May I see your phone?" he asks.

I frown, puzzled, as another fierce burst of gunfire rains

down on the town. I tug my phone out of my pocket and he nods.

I toss it to him with a shrug. "It doesn't have any signal, if that's what you need. Dom has the only sat phone."

"Passcode?" is all he says.

"Six nine six nine," I reply slowly, and his eyes briefly lift in dry disdain before returning to the phone.

Restlessly, I look back down at the town. Fighter after fighter is winking out of view, though that poor woman's agonized screams are still rending the night. Somewhere else, a man bellows for help, and somewhere else again, a window breaks.

Chaos.

It's total chaos.

Is it . . . like this everywhere right now?

"Lucien . . . why is it that you think your parents are safe?"

Jasper's question splits the air like no bullet ever could. Slowly, so slowly, icy cold dread begins to inch through my veins.

My screen glows in his hand, open on my parents' texts.

He didn't want my phone for himself.

"They're . . . you read it. They wanted to go to Vegas. Road trip. So they're . . . they're on the road." My lips feel strangely numb, and this time, that woman's screams make me flinch.

Jasper sighs, nodding to himself. Then he switches the phone off and looks up at me.

"Are they?" he asks softly.

I stare at him.

"Why are you doing this?" I ask, my heart pounding erratically in my ears, and his eyes soften, so much like Beau's when he said *we're dealing with the same thing.*

The woman screams, and I look back at the town, then at Jasper, my throat drying up. That irrational angry panic sparks again, deep in my chest.

Fear is infectious.

I laugh wildly, then shake my head when he doesn't answer. "No, seriously, why are you doing this? Is this helping? Is this helping anyone right now? You think this will help *me*?"

Jasper runs a hand over his mouth, then seems to choose his words carefully. "You don't seem to be grasping the gravity of the situation. I'm concerned that when you do . . . I want to be here, Lucien. For all of you, of course. But . . . I'm here."

"You're not my psychologist anymore, right?" I snap, with more heat than I meant to. I try to force the smile back to my face, but it feels awkward. Wrong. There's too much reckless tension in me. The battle is running too hot. "You retired. Remember?" I swallow hard. "You *left*."

Jasper tips his head back, his jaw flexing as he turns away. "I don't want to argue with you."

Too bad. I feel like a fight.

"So it's okay to press me on my mess, but I can't press you on yours? What were *you* running from, Jasper? Why the hell did you leave like that? You didn't say *anything.*"

I might as well strip naked for how much I'm baring myself, but why not? He *knows* anyway. My throat burns, hot and humiliated.

In the distance, the street war booms.

Then Jasper wheels back around, his eyes catching silvered starlight, intense and overbright. He's angry.

"I had to go, Lucien," he hisses, and fury turns him white to his lips. "This place was a *nightmare* for me, and you will never understand it. I *needed* to go. That wretched job and this awful town. All of it can burn! I'm *done*."

It stabs me, right where I'm aching. He's done with all of us.

Done with me.

I grab the back of my neck, a hard, bitter sound choking out of me. "Well, damn, Jasper. I'm sorry. I didn't realize we were so fucking terrible for you."

Jasper slams a hand on the hood of his car, his face ablaze. "You have no idea what that cost me. To see you every day. To be there, like that, you—"

"What?" Tears spring to my eyes, and I glare down at him. Every single word is another slice. "What did we cost you? Come on, you've come this far. You might as well—"

"You ruined my life," he roars, and all words die in my mouth.

I feel a part of myself die, too, when his eyes shimmer.

Brokenly, he whispers, "I wish I had never met you."

Somewhere, an explosion booms, loud enough to level a building, and we stare at each other as the world comes crashing down around us.

My lips tremble, no matter how I press them together.

His do, too.

A job. I was just a job to him. A job he *loathed*. A job that *hurt* him.

I rub the back of my hand over my mouth, looking away from him. Gutted. I think that's the word for it. Like I've been hollowed out at my very core by some sharp, scraping knife, one that didn't bother to avoid a single nerve on its way out.

Jasper rests my cell phone by my foot, very softly.

Then he braces himself on the hood of his car, exhaling a slow, painful breath.

My head starts to feel light, my own breathing becoming shallow.

I can't think of a single joke. Not even the dirty priest one.

"What the fuck is Beau doing?"

Thomas's shout makes me blink, then whip my gaze back down at the town.

The group that was firing on the pharmacy seems to be down, cleared out by Dom, Jayk, and Beau, but shots are still popping off from inside, and there are more than a dozen other shadows crawling down the street toward it.

That pharmacy is a disaster.

It's too exposed, from too many angles, to be anything but a prime shitshow. Our guys need to bail—we need more asses in gear to even have a hope of securing it.

Except instead of backing away, Beau is sliding in, skidding toward the trash cans while bullets shred the air around him on all sides. He's illuminated by the fire in the next building as he hits the pavement next to her like he's sliding into home plate.

My bleeding heart slams into my throat. The woman screaming, the one that got hit, he's trying to save her.

The trash cans ring as bullets pepper the metal.

Holy shit.

He's doing the hero thing.

I can't make out words, but I hear Jayk shouting. Dom storms out into the middle of the street to cover Beau, spraying bullets above the window line of the pharmacy in a ballsy warn-ing. He's totally exposed, not even firing directly at the civilians inside—any person with a weapon and any training at all would take him out no question.

But they're not trained.

They're scared, angry people who have no fucking clue what they're doing.

At Dom's splattered bullets, the pharmacy goes quiet, and I hear Dom shout—probably at Beau. For a second, I think he's got this.

But then one of the shadows down the street fires.

It's a shitty shot, and Dom steps back sharply as Jayk backs into the street, loosing a string of bullets in the direction of the shot. That goes quiet too, only for another to start up from another angle, until Dom and Jayk are standing back-to-back in the street, protecting each other.

Protecting Beau and whoever is bleeding out on the side of the road.

From this angle, I can see a side service alley about fifteen meters down from the pharmacy. I know this town—it has good booze and a good sense of humor. I've stumbled down these streets more times than I'm proud of, and I could *swear* that alley opens out beside *Give It Your Best Shot*, my favorite grimy darts bar. If they can just get to the alley, they'll be fine. They can take cover there, Beau can do his business, then they can leave out the other end. Maybe steal a Jägermeister for their trouble.

No one wants *them*, after all. They just want the medicine.

But it only takes me a second to see that Dom and Jayk have the wrong angle to see it—and they're too busy fighting off civilians to look.

I leap off the car, running toward town.

"Lucien? What are you doing?" Jasper shouts sharply.

Adrenaline starts chugging through my veins, and I turn around long enough to grin.

"Hero shit!"

There it is.

I flip back around, passing Thomas, and he gives me a startled look.

"Lucky? Fuck. *Stop*, we're on orders to protect the—"

"You protect them. I'm getting our guys," I shout back.

My boots thump over the asphalt, and I click off the safety on my rifle. I pass the fallen utility pole blocking most of the road, climbing over the abandoned car in the other lane to avoid the sparking wires. Action and excitement and fear all surge through my veins, searing me clear of panic. Filling that hollow, hurting cavern.

I'm not made to sit on the sidelines.

Thinking. *Feeling*. Knowing I failed.

I can do all that later. Right now, I need to help my friends. There's a freedom in just being able to *do*.

As I near the town, all the violent, crashing sounds become deafening. Rotten, sulphuric trash and smoky fire burns my nose, and I slow. Training kicks in, and this puzzle almost becomes fun again as I figure out my approach.

How do I get to the alley without accidentally dying?

Sounds like a good board game.

I glance over the bullet-littered streets, over Jayk swearing with a creativity I have to admire and over Dom barking orders at civilians who aren't listening. I skim past burning buildings and around cars ditched in panicked angles across the road, taking it all in until it comes together in my mind.

I need to go wide, come up through the alley from the other side so I can show the others where to go.

I'm creeping around past the darts bar, and I'm almost at

the other end of Rescue Alley when I hear a jagged *crack* behind me.

I whirl around, dropping to a knee and slamming my rifle in place. My finger is over the trigger when Jasper stumbles toward me, cursing.

Blood roars through my ears as I drop my gun.

"What the hell are you doing?" I whisper-shout at him.

Jasper sharply adjusts his shirt like it's personally offended him, glowering at me.

"I'm sure if you gathered all two wits you possess and actually rubbed them together for a change, it *might* spark the understanding that I'm *following* you."

Another wild spray of gunshots splashes the nearby street, and I shoot a glance up the darkened alley. It's dirty and littered with broken beer bottles.

Over me, Jasper is unarmed. Perfectly tailored pants cup his ass like an openmouthed kiss, and dust stains his Manolo loafers. He eyes the dried vomit stains in the gutter with a grimace.

"Why the hell would you do that!" I burst out.

I stand up out of the puddle I knelt in.

I'm half sure it was piss.

Through the alley, I hear Dom booming at Beau to hurry his ass up, and I pause, torn.

Jasper stalks over to me, stepping through the piss puddle like he didn't even see it. "I'm not letting you go running off, half-cocked, all alone. You're going to get yourself killed."

Ugh! Civilians. I swear to fucking God. They see one James Bond movie . . .

My whole body is dancing with the need to move. I don't have time to argue with him. He's here. A pretty, painful liability who thinks I'm the worst thing that ever happened to him.

Let him see me in action for ten minutes.

Let him see more than the baby switch flirting with him from an overstuffed couch.

"No one's getting killed." Burying my frustration, I check my rifle, snapping off the safety, then shoot him a tight, irritated smirk. "And I'm only ever full-cocked, baby."

Jasper gives me a long, decidedly unimpressed grimace, but I'm already sprinting toward the battlefield. When I reach the mouth of it, I edge my shoulder around the brick, peering out as Jasper comes up behind me.

As soon as I do, someone explodes around the corner, slamming into the wall on the opposite side of the alley. A heavy-set man catches himself against the brick, staggering to right himself, then looks up at us with a filthy, frightened face. He sees my gun.

"Please, no, I'm sorry." He backs up before I can say anything, throwing a rattling bag at our feet. He holds his hands up pleadingly, a sob in his voice. "I didn't mean to. Just take it! Take it! Don't shoot!"

I bend down, picking up the bag full of assorted pills. Shit. Beau's going to need this.

Jasper steps forward. "I assure you, sir, we have no intention of—"

The man takes off running down the alley, sending cans scattering down the road, right as the gunfire heats up behind us.

"Beau, get them up! *Move!*" Dom shouts.

Them?

Fuck.

I rip out of the alley to see bedlam. There are civilians behind cars, some crawling down the street. There are people hiding, people shooting, someone fumbling to load a pistol, someone trying to tourniquet their own arm.

From here, I can see Beau behind the Swiss-cheesed trash cans, finishing tying off a blood-bright bandage around a woman's thigh as she tries to hold back her sobs. There's a young girl, maybe three or four, curled up against her chest and squeezing a stuffed bear.

Jayk fires off twice at two men coming toward them, and they shoot back, badly.

He takes several threatening steps forward like a human tank, his skull tattoos twisting over his biceps.

"There's a fucking kid here!" he bellows. He shoots at their feet twice more, then lifts it up to a head shot. "Back the *fuck* off."

One of them jerks back, then drags at the other's arms as they both take off.

They're barely more than kids themselves.

Something crashes from inside the pharmacy, making the little girl squeal and dig into her mama, and that's enough.

I raise my fingers to my lips and whistle sharply.

"Yo! Someone call a tour guide?" I call out to them, and Jayk pivots, locking eyes on me fast. I gesture with my head toward the alley. "Exit's this way, babycakes."

Jayk flips me off, but he whacks Dom on the back and Dom looks our way. Relief breaks over his features.

In moments, he's sliding in beside Beau and they start getting the woman and her kid up—but as soon as he stops shooting, bodies start peeling out of the shadows, sensing their opportunity.

I start firing at the same time as Jayk, warning them back as Beau tugs the little girl off her mother, talking to her soothingly while Dom holds her back. Beau wraps the woman's arm around his neck, and she leans heavily against him, biting her lip piercingly hard, her face scrunched in pain. He starts to drag her forward, but the little girl suddenly abandons her bear to tear free of Dom. She grabs at her mother's dress with fierce, desperate, tiny hands.

"No! Mommy. Don't go! Mommy!"

Dom slings his rifle and scoops up the crying, squirming girl, shielding her in his chest.

Then he runs.

He's unarmed. He and Beau both. And as they take off, the shadowy figures close in on the pharmacy.

Which sets off a brutal burst of return fire from inside.

"Oh dear," Jasper breathes.

I push out further, funneling shots erratically, more to scare the encroaching horde off than anything else. Jayk starts backing toward the alley, following more slowly behind them.

He rings on empty and curses.

Someone comes close to the trash cans, lifting their gun at him, and I fire at the cans, sending a box of old Chinese food splattering across the sidewalk. They reel back again, and Jayk turns and sprints toward me.

Beau is nearing the alley now, but Dom is struggling with the girl, who's thrashing in pure panic.

"My bear! No, Mommy! I want my bear!"

My heart rips as Dom gets her to the alley. She's sobbing like her world is broken. Like something's been taken from her that she's never going to get back. The most important thing she knows.

You just can't take a kid's bear away.

It's family.

As soon as the others are clear, I unsling my rifle, then turn, shoving it into Jasper's arms.

"Lucien, what are you doing?" Jasper's voice is a lash behind me.

"Just a quick trip. It'll take me two seconds," I assure him. "Cover me!"

Jasper's eyes widen, pools of dark panic in his pale face. He looks down at the rifle, fumbling as he turns it. "Stop. Lucien, I don't know how to use this. *Stop*!"

But I'm already backing toward the trash cans. Toward the bear.

"Safety's off, just point and shoot." I consider that, then grin. "Just try to miss me, okay?"

"Lucien! No!" Jasper's shout blisters my ears as I bolt in toward the goal.

Excitement sparkles through my veins, a purpose *filling* me. The girl gets it all. To be safe with everyone she loves. Her mom.

And her damn bear.

The ragged thing sits against one of the bins, some chow mein nestled into its fur.

Bingo.

I skid around a car as bullets crash to my left, one slicing whisper-close next to my cheek. The last half of the pharmacy window shatters open to my right a second later, and I dive to the ground, laughing riotously as sharp, sugary pieces crackle over me.

At this rate, I may lose the "not dying accidentally" game.

I crane my head around, checking on Jasper, to see him let

off an unruly burst of shots ten feet away that makes him stagger back, and I snort into the ground.

Well, he tried.

I look back toward the trash cans and see the bear, one patched eye winking at me from a few feet away. This guy. No way can this ugly cutie get left behind.

People are rushing the pharmacy now, and at least one person steps on my ass as I'm forgotten about. There are a few more distant shots, but they're quickly overtaken by the sounds of wrestling and overturning shelves.

I army crawl forward, until finally, the bear falls into my hands.

The little guy grins up at me.

Sitting up, I laugh again, pure, bright victory flooding me. I fucking did it. Sure, Beau saved a mother and Dom saved a kid, and Jayk saved all of them, but me? *I* saved Patchy. King of Bears.

Now that girl not only gets her ever after, but she gets to be happy in it, too.

I look back down at the alley, but I can't see anyone, not with the angry swarm of people around me who clearly did not get the memo about this momentous moment.

I'm getting to my knees, brushing myself off, when I hear a low, resonant click.

A safety.

The metallic kiss of cold metal at my temple kills my victory vibes fast.

The frantic, shuddery way it clatters against my skin grinds them into the dirt.

Scared people do dangerous things.

"Give me the bag!" a man spits over me, sounding terrified.

Bag? My mind blanks for a split second before I remember the bag of pills the guy threw at me in the alley.

Ohhh, damn.

"Hey, man, it's okay. We're okay. I'm just going to—" I lift my hand toward the strap at my shoulder, and I only have a heartbeat for instinct to tell me to slam myself backwards before he shoots.

The muzzle flashes and the bright imprint almost blinds me. I blink rapidly, my heart racing, my head spinning as I lie on the ground, deafened, the bear in one hand.

Above me, the clouds part just enough to see stars twinkle.

He shot at me.

He's going to—

The gun goes off again, this time the bullet hits a few inches above my head, and the guy kicks me hard as I scramble back. His breathing is erratic, wild, and fear sets in, clutching at my throat.

"The bag!" he screams, shooting again.

I roll to the side as the ground explodes beside me, kicking out, and he staggers, but doesn't drop the gun. He aims it at me again, and all I can see is muzzle.

Oh, shit.

Maybe I am no better at coping than Beau.

Reality hits me, sharp and sweet, and all the shouting and battle noise fades into nothing as I take a last breath.

I'm going to die.

With this bear.

With my parents.

I see the man's mouth move, the unhinged spray of spit on his lips as he shouts again for the bag, but I don't hear it. The shadowed inside of the muzzle of his gun lines up with my eye, but I don't see it.

I only see Jasper leaning toward the glove compartment, his lips a breath from mine.

Then the man's face explodes.

His cheek rips apart, his skull fragmenting, and blood spurts over me and Patchy like an unholy fountain.

A second later, he drops.

Stunned, I look up, and Jasper is still holding the rifle in a white-knuckled grip, his face dead white and stricken as he stares down at the body.

He covered me.

Stiltedly, I get to my feet.

"Jasper?" I ask, my voice a shocky hush.

Slowly, his eyes lift to mine. He's shaking. I take the rifle from him—what he did, what I did, sinking in.

"Oh, God," he whispers.

He killed someone.

He killed someone *for me*.

He killed someone for me because I thought it would be fun to save a stuffed *bear*.

Tears spring to my eyes as people rage around us, and my breath hitches. "You shouldn't have done that. Jasper, fuck, I . . . I shouldn't have . . . I'm sorry."

Running on autopilot, I drag him away, and he follows woodenly until we're under the half-cover of a truck.

"I covered you," he whispers. He presses a hand to his mouth, then drags it down to his throat. He stares at me, his eyes running over every inch of my face, and at the naked terror there, I can't help myself—I grab him, yanking him into a hug.

He freezes.

My heart is thundering, and his is hammering just as bad, but it only takes moments for them to fall into a rhythm. We're alive. He's okay.

My careful, safety-conscious indoor cat. Our glue, the one who keeps us all together when all this shit threatens to break him. The one who is meant to stay good and pure and safe.

I made him a killer.

Slowly, hesitantly, his arms close around me—and then he's hugging me back like he never wants to stop. Close, fierce. He buries his face in my neck, and I feel the heated press of his body all along mine.

"I covered you. Damn it, Lucien, I thought I couldn't. I thought you were going to die while I watched, but I did it. I covered you." The words are mumbled and frantic, and I squeeze my eyes shut. Hot, shameful tears spill out onto his satin shirt.

He killed because of me. He was right about all of it, but I wouldn't listen.

And now I'm ruining his shirt.

He makes a rough, choked sound against my neck, and I want to wither up and die for putting him here like this.

No wonder he wishes he never met me.

"Lucky, get your ass back to the convoy. Thomas needs help clearing a path for the cars!" Dom shouts from somewhere.

But I can't let go of Jasper.

"You covered me. I'm okay," I tell him.

He makes that choked sound again, and I frown, pulling back. Holding him by the shoulders, I try to see his face, wondering if he's having a panic attack.

Jasper brings one hand up, squeezing the bridge of his nose —and he snorts, turning away. My mouth drops open as he clamps his lips shut, only for another wild, bursting laugh to shake free.

"I'm sorry," he gasps, clamping a hand over his mouth. Then he snorts again, bending over at his waist until his hair falls wildly out of its usual composure. His shoulders start shaking. "I'm—"

I blink, then rub the back of my head. The stuffed bear blinks up at me, equally confused.

People have all kinds of reactions to their first kill.

Haven't really seen a giggle fit before, though.

And if you'd asked me who *would* have had a giggle fit after their first, Jasper would be exactly last on that list.

"Um. Did I miss something?" I ask, attempting a smile as another snorting, uncontrolled bout of laughter overtakes him, and Jasper straightens wiping his eyes.

He waves a hand at me—and his smile might be the most beautiful, cursed thing I've ever seen.

"I *covered* you," he repeats. His eyes travel over my hair and my face, then my clothes, and I look down, realizing just now exactly how drenched in blood and brain matter I am.

Ooh, *not* hot.

Then I get it.

"You covered me," I say dryly, and this time we both start laughing. It keeps coming, in rolling, breathless, wheezing waves until tears are flowing over my cheeks, and he steps into me, pressing me against the car.

Then finally, the laughter peters out, and he just looks at me.

After a moment, he pulls out his pretty handkerchief from his pocket and he starts wiping at my cheeks, cleaning away the blood and shame and all the tears.

"You miserable, beautiful, foolish child," he murmurs.

With the back of one finger, I brush his hair back into place.

"It's going to be okay," I whisper. "Even if they're gone. We'll get back to base. You'll be safe."

Slowly, the darkness begins to fall away from his face and a light glows in his eyes. My heart lifts at how pretty it is, how pretty *he* is, for just a moment before the strangeness of it hits.

Jasper's eyes flick over my shoulder, and he straightens, his lips parting.

It shouldn't be this bright.

I whip around just in time to see the whole world turn white.

The world is white.

The imprint of it burns into my retinas, so impossibly bright that I see the skeletons of every stranger around us flash through their skin. My breath suspends, and I clutch Lucien to my chest.

In this beat before death takes us, it's not dying I fear.

Only eternity without him.

Hot air rushes us with violent force, shattering windows and tossing shrapnel with a buffeting roar, and we stagger, braced together against the storm.

This is it. If this is my last moment, if I'm to be stardust and a dream, then let it be with him. Let our dust spin out together. He'll be my dream through every galaxy.

Our hearts will beat their last as one.

His cheek is against mine, pinpricks of stubble piercing me in tiny bites. His lips rest by the hollow under my ear, panting hot, urgent breaths over my skin in carnal symphony—the way he might pant if I were fucking him like this, with him desperate and pinned beneath me, all those glorious muscles made useless by his need.

If I'm to die, I'm dying without knowing what that might feel like.

What those lips might taste like.

How sweetly he might sleep beside me each night.

I get this, though. Even as I feel my skin begin to burn, I have him in my arms.

But . . . that whiteness doesn't sear us into ash clouds. The wind doesn't shred our skin from our bones. I look up to see a mountain of thunderous flames.

It must be the Rangers' base. The blast is miles away, but it engulfs the sky like a fiery god, swallowing the stars. The mush-roomed head belches smoke into the clouds, and the molten glow is still enough to scald my eyes.

The sound hits.

Lucien and I burst apart, and I slam my hands over my ears as the crack of thunder booms, and around us, dozens of others do the same. It presses in on my eardrums like a war hammer, and that column of orange and black death sucks in a raging breath.

It's unbridled.

Vile and ruinous and awesome in its sheer, grotesque power.

The wave of hot wind passes us, sucking away all noise and leaving behind a deafened void that chills my marrow.

Still, that giant, riotous firestorm rises . . . and the earth trembles under our boots.

Slowly, people spill out of the pharmacy, their medicines forgotten as they come to stare until the streets are filled with rows of civilians, lined up in fearful worship. Guns and makeshift clubs hang from their fingertips.

Beaumont takes a shocked step forward, then another, until he's beside us too.

Then Jaykob.

Then Dominic.

"Our base." Dominic's eyes reflect the shooting flames. "The Colonel . . ."

I squeeze my eyes closed for a moment, my heart throbbing in my throat. Even now. Even now he can't call him *Dad*.

Suddenly Dominic shakes his head like he's disagreeing. Like it doesn't make sense. He steps forward again, over the wretched, dusty stuffed bear Lucien almost lost his life for, his eyes searching the blistering light.

"Dom," Beaumont says heavily, catching his shoulder, and Dominic waves him off. "No, Dom, talk to me, we can—"

A small delivery truck peels around a corner, then crashes into the trash cans outside the pharmacy. It slams to a stop, its horn howling, and Beaumont curses, snagging his medical bag. But before he can sprint over, the driver falls out of the truck. He takes one look at the violent fireball on the horizon and bolts.

But I keep my eyes on the captain.

Dominic turns slowly, running a hand over his jaw, taking in the shattered windows and damaged walls, the bullet blasts and the bodies and all the broken mess around us. He looks from terrified civilian to terrified civilian, as they stare at the burning ball of fire bleeding into the night. The overturned utility pole sparking, its wires writhing and snapping over the street.

So much damage in such a short amount of time.

So many people who have no defense against an attack.

His gaze stops.

The injured woman they rescued is crying silently, huddled against a shop wall. Her bandaged leg is a bloodied mess—but she's gripping her struggling little girl with white knuckles, murmuring soothingly to her.

Dominic stares at them with dawning fear, then his gaze whips back to the blast, to where a column of roiling clouds rises, rises . . . until I realize he's not looking at the explosion at all.

Overhead, those blackened clouds crawl out toward us, sludging the sky.

Horrified realization slams into his face, and he looks back at the girl with frozen dread. And it's only as another gust of air buffets me that it finally clicks for me too—why those clouds and that blustery, urgent breeze are so, so terrible.

We're downwind.

We're downwind of a massive irradiated firestorm.

My eyes find Lucien, standing in stricken awe of the distant blaze. Oranges and reds flicker over his gorgeous, bloodstained face.

No.

I might have failed at much in my years. At my marriage, my professional oaths, my own sense of right and wrong. I might have sworn by everything I hold dear that I would never lay so much as a finger on him.

But I didn't kill tonight only for Lucien to die. I sacrificed another human—my own *soul*—for him today. He might need to live in another country to keep me from breaking my oaths, but he *will* live.

Lucien's life is bought and paid for.

But if he's to live, we need orders, and Dominic's breathing has shallowed, his eyes sightless as the same understanding I've reached takes him. There's no base. No backup. No military or intel or colonels to save us now.

There's only him.

Dominic and his team, who would follow their captain into that very inferno if he so asked.

There's also me.

I can't sling guns or drop from planes. My job doesn't require me to risk my life—but it does require me to keep my head. To remain calm and to *think*, no matter what I see or hear. No matter what I feel.

I need to do my job, so that they can do theirs.

"What are your orders, Captain?" I ask him, cool and professional.

"Give him a fucking minute, Jasper. His parents were in there," Beaumont snaps, shoving me away from Dominic. He's charged with fear and anger and adrenaline, the shadows of everything he's lost today darkening his usual charm.

But already I taste metal at the back of my throat. The air is beginning to burn, becoming acrid and electrical.

My pulse trembles at the taste of death, but I lift my chin and stare Beaumont down.

We don't *have* a fucking minute.

Dominic's gaze breaks from the woman and her child. He stares at me hard, ignoring Beaumont, and finally, his head tips back. I can almost see the moment the captain's duty settles heavily on his shoulders.

There it is.

I murmur, "Readily will I display the intestinal fortitude required to fight on to the Ranger objective and complete the mission . . ."

" . . . . Though I be the lone survivor." He finishes the Ranger's Creed with a low, resolute finality.

"Rangers lead the way," I say softly, and he meets my eyes.

And finally, he inclines his head.

It's his promise. His soul. The only prayer his father ever sent him to bed with.

I nod back, relieved. "These people need to be seen to safety, Captain—and you're the highest ranking official here. We need orders."

"Dom . . ." Beaumont starts, but Dominic's shoulders firm, and he bends down, swooping up the girl's filthy bear from under his feet.

"The Colonel knew the job, Beau." He straightens, brushing off some of the dirt from a matted ear. "And so do I."

Without waiting for his friend's response, he strides over to the woman and her child, then he kneels beside them.

He lifts the bear.

The girl's teary eyes light up, enough to clear the skies, and she swipes at the snot streaking her grubby face. "Look, Mommy, my bear! The man has my bear!"

Her mother is only half conscious, and tears streak through the dust on her pain-drenched face, but she works up a tight, tremulous smile for her daughter.

"Thank you." Her words for Dominic are a choked whisper.

His jaw flexing, Dominic hands the girl the bear . . . and she beams.

She beams like she doesn't understand that the world is about to sicken and die. The little girl doesn't know that more bombs will come. That soldiers may even now be ripping through our towns, murdering our men and plundering our resources. That perhaps people closer to home are doing some ripping themselves. For this girl, hope only needs to extend as far as her mother . . . and that bear.

But the mother knows.

Silent, hopeless tears slip over her cheeks as her daughter dances on her toes, clutching that stuffed creature the same way I clutched Lucien to myself just minutes ago.

Dominic watches the child with dark concern.

But it's the captain who looks back at her mother.

"No one else is dying today," he promises, and the woman swallows.

She searches Dominic's face desperately—and whatever she sees there makes her hopeless expression break. On a sob, she squeezes her eyes shut and nods.

Grim determination bricks Dominic's face as he gets to his feet. "Jayk, Lucky. We need to move!"

He strides over as Jaykob whacks Lucien's shoulder, startling him out of his awed stare.

"I— Yeah . . . right." He looks up, frowning at the lightning crashing through the encroaching clouds. The very air groans, and Lucien pales. "Shit. How long have we got till that comes down?"

"Do I look like a fucking Geiger counter?" Jaykob snaps, and when several people turn around to look at him with wide, terrified eyes, he scowls at them. "We've got shit flying at us and windows shattering at thirty miles out—we're already too fucking close."

As if in answer, the raging inferno groans again, vomiting more clouds into the sky.

The low murmurs around us pick up into panicked questions, and civilians begin pushing at each other as they try to move in every direction. Something breaks inside the pharmacy, and I grimace.

This is disintegrating, just like at Darkside.

"Evac center is on the south side of town," Dominic says, urgent, but low enough not to be heard by the civilians around us. "It's FEMA-built, last few years, so it should be stocked and big enough to cover everyone. Maybe thirty minutes on foot."

Beaumont looks at the sky. "We have time for that?"

"Look around. You think any of these buildings are secure against fallout? That blast fucked this town," Dominic replies impatiently. "We're out of options. These people need to haul ass."

"On it," Jaykob mutters.

In seconds he's storming toward the surrounding people, his boots crunching on broken glass. "Everyone move! South side of town." He pushes a man standing in the middle of the road forward. "*Go!*"

A few people jump into startled motion. Several others blink at him, illuminated by violent, flickering light, and Jaykob stalks up between them like a human bulldozer.

"Get your ass to the bunker or die shitting blood," he bellows at an elderly man with a cane.

A few shouts go up at that, but the crowd starts to move, pushing toward the evac center in a hurried horde.

"You want to choke on your own vomit? Move!" he booms.

"He has such a gentle touch," Lucien says fondly.

"Where's Thomas?" Beaumont asks, ignoring him, and I look away from the horrifying spectacle of Jaykob on a mission. "We have injured here—they can't walk and carrying them will take too long."

"So we need wheels." Dominic nods his agreement.

"There." Lucien throws his chin toward the road behind us, where the fallen utility pole still blocks half of the street, and a chunky sedan blocks the other half. Snaking, sparking wires writhe over the asphalt.

The convoy is stalled along the winding road, waiting for the path through to be cleared.

Thomas and two other Darkside members try to lift the sedan onto its side—until one of the electrical wires snaps up, sending them shying back. My heart pounds. One wrong move and they'll be fried.

Another foul-tasting gust whips past us, and Beaumont meets my eyes.

His fear matches mine.

"There are other ways into town, aren't there?" Lucien asks anxiously. "Should they go around? Meet us there?"

"Then we lose the injured," Beaumont argues, keeping his voice low. "I can see over a dozen here who can't walk. I'm not leaving them here."

"We're not leaving anyone. Lucky, help Thomas. Get them moving," Dominic snaps. "They need to go faster. We don't have time."

Lucien nods, unusually serious, and before I can offer my assistance, he takes off at a run, shoving people out of the way and whistling sharply to the convoy.

"Beau, get the injured into one place. We can file them in as the cars come through." Dominic's eyes flick to me. "Help him."

"Of course," I murmur, though my gaze still lingers on Lucien as he tries to approach the lashing, sparking wires.

That boy has as much caution as he has sense.

Which is to say, *none*.

But in this, I need to trust him.

Dominic takes off in the other direction, helping Jaykob push people down the street, dragging them away from their looting with whipcrack orders until the civilians are moving at a jog toward the evacuation center. Until only the blaring horn of the crashed truck fills the street.

The sky darkens, and Beaumont and I work as quickly as we can to help injured civilian after injured civilian, moving them to sit beside the woman and her daughter so we can take care of the worst injuries as best we can. There are broken bones, burns, crush wounds from damaged buildings, and deep cuts from shattered glass. People blinded by the blast, or torn apart by gunfire, and a few others simply weeping over bodies that Beaumont covers with solemn sadness and then moves on from.

And all the while, those thick, greasy clouds reach out their charred fingers.

"We're taking too long," I mutter.

"God damn it," Beaumont curses, moving the last person against the wall. Sweat stains his shirt.

Lucien and Thomas and the two other men have moved around to another angle, trying to avoid the wires—but they can't seem to get enough leverage to roll the car.

"Mommy, it's raining!"

"Eleanor, get back over here, *now*!" the mother snaps.

Something brushes my cheek and I touch it, then look up. Snowflakes of debris are falling. A delicate frond of silver dust lands on Beaumont's arm and he touches it. As soon as his fingertip makes contact, it crumples.

He pales, looking up at me with stark eyes, and dread collects in my stomach.

People are wailing in pain, weeping and pulling away from

the fallout . . . and Lucien is still in the middle of the street, the dust collecting in his hair.

I flinch.

That car needs to move *now*.

Stepping forward, I rack my brain—the angles are wrong, they're never going to lift it from there, even with me and Beaumont helping. They can't get under it. But the utility pole is too large to move, those wires too dangerous. We need distance. Leverage. We need . . .

My eyes land on the crashed delivery truck, its horn still shouting from the center of the road like its demanding attention.

We need a truck.

Dominic and Jaykob jog up behind us.

"The path still isn't cleared?"

"The fuck are they doing?"

I run.

"Jasper!" Dominic snaps.

I reach the truck in seconds and yank open the door. Sliding into the front seat, I let out a relieved—perhaps slightly hysterical—laugh when I see the keys still in the ignition.

That god-awful driver just became my new favorite human.

My hands shake as I turn the keys—partly with hope, but mostly with fear. I'm built for air-conditioned offices and chess games. This sort of thing is foolish. Reckless, even. And with those wires sizzling the road? It's certainly dangerous.

It's something Lucien might do.

Incredibly, right now, the thought is strangely thrilling.

My pulse thundering in my throat, I back the truck up fast, turning it through the street and it squeals to a halt beside the group of men trying to heave the car onto its side.

And leaning over the filthy window, I raise one disparaging brow. "As impressive as this phenomenal display of testosterone is . . . perhaps you might consider an alternate solution?"

The car slams down.

Panting, Lucien wipes the sweat from his brow and looks up at me. Deathly ash falls around him, but he doesn't pay it any mind.

Instead, he smiles at me.

It's a slow, devastating turn of his wicked lips, and those sinful, impish dimples wreck me, bring me to my knees, just as they've done from the moment he first walked into my office.

"Now who's cocky?" he teases, and I can't help my soft smile back.

Then Thomas is looking for chains, and the men are securing them in as many places as they can manage, hooking up the truck to the sedan for a makeshift tow. If this works, we can avoid the wires entirely.

If this works, we'll all make it.

Suddenly, the ground rumbles as down the street, a building crumbles with a resonant *crash*.

Everyone pauses for a moment, watching the cloud of dust scatter, then Thomas booms, "Go, Jasper! Move!"

My hands clench on the steering wheel, and I ease my foot onto the accelerator.

Please, please, please.

The truck groans, the wheels skidding, and for a taut, breathless moment, I think it will work. That we'll clear the way. That the injured waiting for their rescue won't be forced to swallow poison instead of air. That my friends from Darkside won't be stuck, coffined in their cars, as toxic rain corrodes the metal around them.

That Lucien's skin won't sizzle and peel away with the acid drip of rain.

One of the chains flings off the truck with a loud *twang* and Thomas ducks to avoid it, but I ignore it all, focusing only on my foot and that accelerator.

Because, for a moment, I have hope.

The truck lets out a metallic screech, like it's ripping apart, and sweat beads along my hairline, desperation searing me.

Please.

"Stop! Stop!" someone shouts. "You'll burn the transmission!"

The hope dies.

I take my foot off the accelerator and brace myself against the wheel, my breathing fast and panicked as our failure hits me.

"Can we get the injured to the convoy instead?" Lucien replies desperately. "Get them to go another way?"

"Around the wires? Up that slope?" Thomas blows out a breath. "Maybe a few, if all of us help. But the time . . ."

"Screw the time. We do that. We'll make it work."

Outside, the debris begins to fall faster, and I close my eyes.

We're done. It's too late.

We're going to die.

Maybe today, or maybe in a few weeks or months when sickness takes us, but we can't withstand this level of fallout, not for long. We don't have time.

But I know the Rangers won't leave anyone behind . . . and I won't leave them.

Surrender is not a Ranger word.

We'll get as many up to the convoy as we can. We'll carry them until our skin blisters and our throats swell.

"Just back *up*. Do any of you know a fucking thing about cars?"

Jaykob's irritated voice startles me out of my hopelessness, and my eyes lift to the rearview mirror. He stalks in, his face an impatient wall, and he shoves Thomas out of the way to peer into the car.

"Goat-brained fucking idiots." He scowls. "You can't tow shit with it like this. It's sitting in park, you dumb bimbo assholes."

"Dude, no keys," Lucien snaps back.

Rolling his eyes, Jaykob yanks his pistol out of its holster and shoots out the driver-side window. The alarm goes wild, but he only reaches in and unlocks the door with a scathing, pointed look at Lucien. He holsters his gun and tugs out his pocketknife—then lets himself into the car.

When Jaykob gets out again, he slams the door. "Just put the fucker in neutral next time."

Lucien stares at him with wide, incredulous eyes. "Okay, Grand Theft Auto."

"Have you got it?" Dom shouts. It's more of a demand than a question.

"Got it!" Thomas calls back.

The car rolls forward a fraction of an inch, and Lucien freezes, excitement spilling over his face. "No, okay, you *do* have it! Holy shit, that was awesome! Show me how? Jayk? Please? I *need* to know how to do that." Then he pauses, sliding Jaykob a sideways look. "How *do* you know how to do that?"

Jaykob swipes a snowflake of debris off his head and mutters, "Some of us shoved leotards up our assholes while we were teenagers, some of us worked on cars."

"When you say 'worked on,'" Lucien starts, but Jaykob slaps the roof of the car and turns back to me.

"Move, Jasper. It'll go."

Hope catches in my chest.

Beside Dominic and Beaumont, the civilians are watching us fearfully as I put the truck back into drive.

Please.

This time, when I push my foot down onto the accelerator, the car doesn't scream like it's ripping apart. Metal chains creak, windshield wipers slide through the smattered debris, and the wheels skid, hiss, then . . .

They *catch*.

Suddenly, the truck eases forward, and my heart soars. It worked. It *worked*!

There's resistance, and it's slow, but foot by foot, I drag the car out of the way. I drag it until the road is clear and the next deafening roar isn't from the thunderous aftershocks of a nuclear bomb.

It's from the civilians.

A chorus of horns from the convoy goes up in a riotous cheer, and the waiting group holler their happiness, clutching each other through tears.

In the street, Dominic and Beaumont are whooping, the bomb cloud at their back. Jaykob sticks two fingers in his mouth, whistling in triumph as Thomas laughs and slaps his shoulder.

My eyes sting with relief.

Through my window, Lucien looks only at me, alight with joy.

We're going to *live*.

I let the others release the chains from the truck, then I pull up by the group of injured civilians, the first in line. Behind me, the convoy begins to wind into town.

It happens quickly after that.

In Jaykob's truck, Thomas leads the convoy while we work to help civilians into vehicles. They help each other, holding out supportive arms and steadying injuries as they squeeze too many people into crowded seats. Beaumont finally climbs into the bed of his truck with two of the injured, and Dom drives them out.

And then it's just me and Jaykob standing in the street, blankets we took from the cars wrapped over our heads and covering our mouths. The sky falls around us in black and grey.

As we wait for Lucien, Jaykob stares back at base. At the clouds that will be stamped in my mind for the rest of my life.

"You didn't suck today," he finally mutters.

From Jaykob?

A surprising flush of quiet pride fills me, and I slide a soft, amused glance his way. "I believe you called me a bimbo?"

Jaykob snorts. After a moment, he shrugs. "Whatever. Heat of the moment. Not like it's true." My Volvo pulls in beside us, and his rough face kicks into a smirk as he squeezes in beside my marble bust. "Bimbos are hot."

Rolling my eyes, I get in, detangling the blanket from my head, and Lucien searches my face. "Are you . . . You're okay?"

Those blue eyes are brilliant, fringed with lashes the darkest shade of blond. I should pull away—the thought stirs in the back of my mind—but it's instantly lost under that wave of blue. Under the trembling, joyous relief that quakes my nerves.

"I'm fine, Lucien, I'm . . . I'm wonderful."

A hint of a blush singes his cheeks, but his smile kicks up, cocky and warm. "Yeah. You are."

I blink, startled, studying him as my pulse suddenly skids.

He's confident. Blatantly, shamelessly flirting with me like he has the right to. Like he's *mine*.

I can't have him, not in any living world, but . . . I don't want to ruin it yet. Not when his eyes are shining and victory lights my veins. Not with his forearm flexing, tattooed and muscled and entirely too dangerous in the safe predictability of my car.

Just for a moment, I can indulge it. Just once.

"You were wonderful, too, you know," I murmur.

And, finally, our eyes catch.

"What am I? Dog shit?" Jaykob mutters from the backseat. "I'm fine, too. Thanks for asking."

I shift back into the passenger seat, sucking in a breath.

Composure.

I'm sure I have it somewhere.

Lucien chokes out a laugh, looking up in his mirror. "Glad you're safe too, buddy."

The wretched brat grins then, and his fingers dance on my wheel. "Now, please strap yourself in for the slowest getaway on record. Keep all arms and legs inside the vehicle and do *try* not to panic," he mocks as I fastidiously fasten my seatbelt. "This thing is basically a mechanical roll of bubble wrap anyway."

"You truly cannot help yourself, can you?" I mutter.

His grin widens, and he tosses me a considering look. "You ever opened this granny up to see what she can do?"

I freeze. "*No*, Lucien."

The rogue winks.

In the next instant, he's slammed down on the accelerator and is peeling down the street, the arrow on the speedometer rising higher, higher. *Higher.*

I clutch at the side of the car, scrambling for purchase as he skids, screeching around a corner, laughing like he's taken leave of his senses.

"Lucien! *Stop!*"

In the backseat, Jaykob snorts. "We're barely hitting eighty."

We barrel down the next long road, faster and faster, until Beaumont's red truck comes into view ahead of us, Beaumont in the bed, covered in blankets.

Lucien veers sharply into the next lane, bringing us up beside the truck, and Dominic tosses me a tight, alarmed look. I glower back at him.

As if this is *my* fault.

"Hey, maybe you can street race with this thing after all. Reckon we can beat them there?" Lucien asks, already pulling ahead.

Dominic glares incredulously at me as we pass.

"Dom isn't going to race you, dipshit," Jaykob drawls.

And Lucien shrugs fatalistically. "Won't be much of a race then."

"Lucien! I did not survive a nuclear blast only for you to drive us into a wall!" I snap as he swerves wildly around some fallen debris.

"Jasper, Jasper, Jasper. Have some faith!"

He is far too cheery.

We roar down the street as the rain starts to come down harder, and I fantasize about all the ways I would take this out on his hide if I were to have him alone. Scalding hot wax to the soles of his feet. Safety codes lightly cut into his skin until he's slicked with blood. His balls in a vice that would turn that smugness into the same needy, shuddering mess he became tonight, from just watching my show.

Lucien would take all of it.

He would tend my cock, let me bury myself in that perfect mouth, just to appease me.

He would—

The heavy metal gate's appearance at the end of the street is breathtakingly sudden.

"Lucien, the gate won't open. Lucien, slow down," I snap.

It's already too close. He can't slow in time. I curl in on myself as the thick metal wall looms too large, too near. We're going to—

Lucien spins my car to the side, slamming on the breaks, and we slide out to a stop . . . and the Volvo lightly kisses the gate.

It takes me a full minute to decide I did not, in fact, release my bowels.

Lucien cackles from the driver's seat, and Jaykob smacks the back of my head.

"Stop whimpering. We're here."

Shaking, stilted, I unlock myself from my protective curl, and Lucien's irreverent grin greets me.

"You okay?" he asks sympathetically.

Drawing in a steady breath, I adjust my clothes. "The punishment that you deserve . . ."

Despite the tight, ferocious threat, Lucien's grin widens.

Perhaps even because of it.

But when I look up, I see the wide gate, still just as intimidating. "HOWARDS EVACUATION CENTER" is written above it. The blanket back over his head, Jaykob pounds on the metal.

"The other cars aren't here," I say.

"It's fine. Less lines here. It's just—"

With a loud, electric hiss, the gate opens, and relief floods me as Jaykob ducks inside.

"The back way." Lucien tosses me another wink as he opens his door. "It's my favorite."

Ceaseless brat.

I follow him out, then through the gate and into the evacuation center.

The doors close behind us, and we're greeted by a wide, concrete atrium and multiple people in full hazmat suits who ask us to remove and discard our clothes under blinding fluorescent lights.

In only our undergarments, they direct us into a shower room where Jaykob is naked and scrubbing himself with a narrow bar of soap.

"Ooh, friends shower. Cute," Lucien remarks, stripping off so quickly that I couldn't have missed the toned, tanned flex of his ass if I'd tried.

There goes the next decade of sleep.

Resisting the urge to stare, I pivot, then stride over to the far end of the room to shower myself. As the water hits me, I close my eyes and force memories of the horrifying inferno back into my mind. Anything to dislodge the imprint of that perfect ass, and the cruel, lickable dimples at the base of his spine.

I refuse to sport an erection for *friends shower.*

Just minutes later, we're offered towels and fresh clothes, and they hand us back our cleansed belongings. We're taken through a medical bay for a brief assessment, given medicine that tastes like sour milk, advised that we're required to remain for a minimum forty-eight hours for our own safety . . . and then we're allowed to descend into the general bunker.

It's enormous, deep under the earth, encasing hundreds of

people in thick, impenetrable concrete. There are tunnels like rivers branching out from the main room, but most of the civilians are gathered together, checking on friends and holding loved ones. Some people are crying, sitting on their own, but few are left for long before they're offered food, or someone simply sits beside them.

It's a bustle of motion and the cavernous room is full to the brim with wonderful, heartfelt chatter. So many people who made it to safety. All of them *alive*, while only death lies above.

It's still not enough.

This room could hold three hundred more and not feel the strain. My mind can't stretch around how many people have died today, in this state alone. I can't, right now, find more than a dull, tired horror at the magnitude, or bear a thought for how many more we might have rescued had we been faster, smarter, or better prepared. How many more people could be filling this room right now, had things been different. It's not enough.

But it's something.

The Darkside members are sitting on a stage on the far left of the room, eating packaged rations together under the glowing golden lights. The injured we rescued are safely in the medical bay, being tended by people who have the means and skills to help them, at least for now.

And as I see the mother and her daughter in the arms of a weathered-faced man, it doesn't feel like we did *something* today.

It feels like we did everything.

Thick, hot emotion fills my throat, the release of tension almost enough to take me out at the knees, and then . . . a firm hand slips into mine.

I look down as Lucien's fingers run over my palm, then

twine between my own. My eyes snap up to his face, and he's looking over at me with such a searching, open vulnerability that mortified heat scorches my cheeks.

That look is offensively transparent, questioning and intense, and I force my eyes from him . . . lest he see the same in me.

Because if we're not, in fact, dying, then separation is very much required.

It's the only reason I'm here at all, divorced and unemployed, packed and retreating as swiftly as possible to my summer home, Bristlebrook, all dignity long abandoned.

Then again, if I hadn't been trying so desperately to run from this impossible, beautiful twenty-four-year-old *child*, I likely would have been soundly asleep in my bed, back on that very base that's now smearing the sky.

Instead, my kind, lovely ex-wife is likely dead in her new lover's home in Houston.

My heart aches bitterly for her loss. Soomin gave me so much understanding—for my sadism, and for the damned love she saw blooming in me, no matter how I tried to hide it. She understood me, even as she decided she deserved better for herself.

She was right.

Soomin deserved better than me.

She deserved better than to die a year later, after finally finding someone who could appreciate her for the wonderful woman she was.

And Lucien deserves better than being preyed upon by his psychologist—a man fourteen years his senior, no less.

So rather than closing my fingers around him as I so desperately want to do . . .

I let him go.

Stepping back, I tuck my burning hand behind my back and look over to the stage, where Thomas and the other Dark-side members sit.

"We should check in with Thomas," I say softly.

"Right," Lucien breathes, looking away from me. He swallows, his fingers curling in.

"Right," he repeats, more softly.

I know every flavor of pain. Every chord. So I know exactly how many strings of it I just plucked in him. I can hear the sonata ringing in that word. It rings sharply enough to cut me through and slice apart my victorious glow.

But it's for the best.

Our kind of love is for dreams and stardust. For eternities on the wind. It doesn't belong to the living.

There are far too many ways I would hurt him here.

Jaykob comes up beside us, tugging at his pants. "These clothes are riding up my asshole. Who did they think was surviving this shit? Tinkerbell?"

Lucien huffs a laugh, but it doesn't sound right. It has too many notes of hurt.

He walks off, heading toward Thomas, and I follow more slowly behind, trying to regather myself.

It's for the best. I'll leave for Bristlebrook as soon as we're released. We'll be free of one another for good.

It doesn't make me feel any better.

"What? They riding his ass too?" Jaykob mutters.

I purse my lips, choosing to ignore that, and climb the stairs to the stage. The Darkside members welcome us warmly, if tiredly, sharing food and threadbare pleasantries. Phill's nether appendage is apparently still intact, and not shot off by his own weapon. Hallie rests quietly beside Katie, whose skin is still tender and raw under her shirt.

I scan the room, not seeing Dominic or Beaumont.

"The other entrance. To your left," Lucien says quietly, and it's an effort not to give him a sharp look, my heart thudding at how he watches me.

Instead, I look to my left and see Beaumont, tall and exhausted and freshly clothed in the same nauseous green sweats as we are. Jaykob whistles, and he spots us, his face relaxing.

As he walks over, Dominic comes through the doors behind him . . . and he's holding an apple pie.

Everything in me aches. Beaumont's mother was famous for her apple pie, all across base. I'm half sure even the Colonel would have handed over America's secrets for a single slice.

And now there's only one left in the world.

They sit down, joining us without fuss, and I lean back against the wall of the stage, looking at each one of them in turn.

Alive. We're alive.

All of us are quiet. Exhaustion and relief and heavy thoughts don't lend well to small talk, but I see the relief. The fear. The horror and the wonder as they look over the room at all the civilians we saved, and all of those who saved themselves.

Dominic finally lets out a long, heavy breath, his head dropping into one hand. "All these people. We have nothing. No protection. No firepower. No intel. If it's war . . ." He shakes his head. "We've already lost."

The grave, unspeakable elephant crushing the room.

"We keep them safe," Thomas says, watching Dominic from across our circle. "Just like we did tonight. It's what we're built for. We just . . . if we do anything, we do that." Thomas tosses a packaged ration of food over to him and smiles grimly. "I've got your back too, Cap. No matter what."

Jaykob stops wrenching at his pants, and his eyes glitter fiercely. "There are other armories. The weapons cache at training camp. The excursion area. Doubt they were hit. They'll be a bitch to get into, but there's plenty of shit in those."

"Ooh, count me in for B&E." Lucien grins, some of the shadows drawing back from his face, and I ache at the sight of fresh sunshine.

In the bunker I hear dozens of voices swirling through the air. Low music. Crying and fear, but also incongruous laughter. A mess. A beautiful, lovely mess.

Beaumont almost smiles, too. "There's medicine here, and I have some supplies. We can hit hospitals. Pharmacies. They'll probably be as much of a bitch fight as the one tonight, but nothing we can't handle."

"We'll do what we can." Dominic considers the others grimly. "But it all means nothing without a base."

Beaumont nudges his shoulder, throwing him a rebuking frown. "We'll figure it out."

We. The word sticks to me. We, as in, them and me. We as in, Lucien, me, and the others.

My plan only involves myself and my Volvo and my solitary penance at Bristlebrook. I can't bring Lucien there, I *can't*. It's my one, final refuge.

I could never resist him. Not when it's just him and me, alone together at the end of the world.

No, I need to give him to Dominic. Let him keep my Lucien safe, as he has done for the past four years.

"We give them hope," Lucien says softly, looking up at

Dominic. His blue eyes glow. "No matter how bad things are, people need hope. We'll find a base, Cap. We'll do it, and we'll save everyone we can along the way. We'll make it right for them."

I *can't*.

I let my head tip back as emotion takes me by the throat. He's too hopeful, too endlessly optimistic for how this will end. I can't do it—think about all the tomorrows and the hopeless inevitability of all of it.

"Tomorrow," I say quietly, lifting my head. "Tomorrow you have time for plans and worries and what comes next. Today, right now, there's no one else to save. There's nothing else to do but rest. And to grieve." I look at each one of them in turn, and one by one, they sober. Lucien can't look at me at all, and it lances my heart. "We've all lost too much today, and we need . . . we need a moment." My words stick. "I don't know if we'll get another."

Beaumont sucks in a harsh breath, his head dropping, and Dominic brings a hand over his back. Jaykob's jaw flexes as he looks away, folding in on himself.

When Beaumont looks up again, his face is reddened, and tears slip over his face. It's not a pretty cry. He sniffs wetly, but he doesn't wipe the tears away.

He picks up the pie, peeling off the wrappings. Fragrant, brilliant cinnamon pours over our group, and he forces a damp smile.

"Mama wanted me to share," he says, then looks up, blinking. "I don't have a knife."

Suddenly, I'm blinking too.

Crying—for his mother, and my own, somewhere across

the world in Seoul. Either with my father, frantically trying to contact me—or in danger herself.

Jaykob pulls out his pocketknife, the one that never leaves his side . . . and he hands it to Beaumont. Beaumont takes it, and I grimace.

"You could wash—"

"You could shut up," Jaykob growls, and I sigh.

Fine. Let us eat with the caveman's stabbing stick. How delightful.

Beaumont carves up six slices and hands them out to us, his breathing shaky.

When the perfect golden triangle hits my hands, my chagrin fades. He's given us a piece of his home, the *last* pieces. I can't imagine how much this pie meant to him—and how much it means that he's giving it to us.

Jaykob takes a shark-like bite of the pie, and I lay a hand on his arm. He stops, then glowers at it.

"To Beaumont's mother, and to his family," I say, lifting the pie. "May God rest their souls."

Jaykob's scowl dies. After a moment, he nods. Beaumont looks down for another long minute, then meets my eyes gratefully. His are red-rimmed. He lifts the pie and takes a bite, and Dominic squeezes his shoulder.

"To the Colonel," the captain says. "My mother. And all the soldiers and their loved ones on base. They lost their lives trying to save us all. God rest their souls."

Everyone takes a bite.

The apple is sweet and a little tart, the crust buttery and sugared. It was made with love, and it falls apart over my tongue like a fond farewell.

It aches everywhere.

Beside me, Lucien is crying too, very quietly.

I stare at the silken, silvered streaks on his face. Carve them into my brain. I want nothing more than to hold him now, to do everything in my power to ease that pain, but I won't.

This must be part of my penance—watching Lucien hurt.

"To my folks," Lucien says next, biting his lip hard. When he releases it, he chokes out a laugh. "Mom never got to shoot that ping pong out of her hoo-ha."

Beaumont snorts, surprised, then laughs, and Thomas rubs the back of his neck.

"Now there's a visual."

I sigh through a dry, sad smile, remembering his texts. Lucien winks, but his lashes are tangled and wet.

Everyone takes another painful bite.

"To all the families everywhere we couldn't save," Thomas says.

"And all the people who have no one to save them from what comes next," Jaykob adds bitterly, and the air becomes heavy and grim.

The next bite is more sour than sweet.

And then, it's me.

I look at the pie in my hands, hurting in more ways than I ever thought, in all my years of training, that it was possible to hurt.

"To my parents. I hope they're safe, and that the whole world hasn't gone as mad as ours has." My bare ring finger shouts at me, the one Lucien noticed in mere moments alone with him. The one that ignited his little spark of hope. I feel his eyes on me now, and shame coats my insides. "And to Soomin, and all the ways I failed her."

When I eat my last bite of pie, it tastes of stinging salt.

I feel a shoulder settle against mine as Lucien moves next to me. Comforting me still, though I rejected him just minutes ago. He doesn't do anything else, just sits there and eats his pie and cures all the world's hurts with his presence alone.

And I know what I need to do.

I knew the moment I stepped foot inside this bunker.

There's no escaping Lucien anymore. There's no more running—at least not in the physical sense. I can't go alone to Bristlebrook and leave them to fight the world's battles for me. I can't live knowing Lucien is elsewhere, in danger.

We all need to be safe. If we're going to survive this, if there's even a chance, then we're all going to need to draw on our strength, more than we've ever had to summon.

Slowly, I pull my wedding ring out of my pocket. I haven't been able to part with it, nor the fear and shame that cling to the silver.

Someone from Darkside laughs, and I look up. Hallie kisses Katie's nose, and Katie laughs again, a blush splashing her cheeks. In the room, people are breathing, talking, living. Sharing food and comfort and love.

Today was a dark day. It's stained with violence and terror and more death than should ever be possible.

But there was good in it too.

Dominic still has his arm on Beaumont's shoulder, and Thomas and Jaykob are shoving one another with reckless grins. Lucien is still firmly by my side, and my despair starts to fall away.

There was courage and strength in our people today.

There was courage and strength in *me* today.

And it's because of them.

Lucien is right. There is hope, and I need to believe in it. I need to believe that the good in our world will win out. That together, we can be more than we are alone.

Because if the good in our world can win out, then perhaps the good in me can win out too. Perhaps, with my friends lending me their strength, I can be the man I always should have been. One who does what's right. Who is there for his people, for *Lucien*, in a way that only helps and causes no harm.

"I know a safe place we can go," I say, and as five heads turn my way, I slide my wedding ring back on my finger.

A reminder of my broken promises, and all the reasons for them.

But also . . . it's a reminder of today. Of the good in me winning out.

I smile softly, enjoying the thought.

"It's my sanctuary, my comfort and peace. It's my Eden." I look over each of them. Dominic and Beaumont, Thomas and Jaykob . . . and Lucien.

Calm fills me.

It might be the end of all things, but at least now, I'll end it with friends.

"We go to Bristlebrook."

Episode Six

Eden

I slip in and out of dreams.

I'm nestled in feather-soft beds. Walking through grand libraries. Sparring with roguish kings. Each time it changes, I'm secreted away somewhere magical. Somewhere safe. It's warm in the otherworlds. I slip between misty fairylands and rest on quiet, stony riverbeds. They're painted in rosy, cozy colors that make no sense, but they soothe me anyway.

But something always tugs me away.

The edges of my dreams are hazy, ephemeral. I want to clutch at the warm, pretty moments with both hands, but when I reach out, I only send them spinning.

They change as they spin.

Lurid. Dark. My dreams twist, coming in nightmarish flashes and screaming bursts as they turn and turn.

The spinning stops.

In a sharp flash, my peaceful riverbed runs red, and Henry stands over the severed head of a pig, his mouth painted crimson, his eyes blank. Blood leaks from the pig's torn, gaping throat into the water. Sluggish red raindrops that drip.

And drip.

And drip.

My white face wavers over the blooming, bloodshot surface.

Drip.

My reflection ripples and suddenly corpse after bloated pig corpse is staring up at me in terror from under the water, their eyes screaming for help.

Drip.

The river ripples again and then the pigs have glasses. They have glasses and long, dark hair that bobs under the bloody waves. They're not pigs at all. They're . . . *Oh God*. They're . . .

My ex-husband's blank, dead stare turns my way.

Tears slip over my nose. Dawning, sucking horror holds me in place.

It's too late.

Henry opens his mouth and it's an empty cavern. A black and endless abyss. His eyes are stark and wide as he draws in a death-rattling breath, preparing to scream, and it sucks in the riverbed too. The world tilts—*I* tilt—and everything slides toward that mouth. Toward that gaping, infinite nothing.

I fall through my own reflection.

Muddy river water fills my veins. It gushes into my throat and streams through my nose. It leaks from my eyes until I can't see. I can't breathe. I'm going under, drowned and dying as I swirl into the dark.

Henry wails as he swallows me. He wails and wails and—

I clutch my throat, gasping back a scream as I sit up.

It's so black, so impossibly dark when I open my eyes that my first thought is that he consumed me whole. That I've been sucked away to nowhere.

I'm lost in nightmares.

But then I blink, then blink again, disoriented in time and space. Slowly, the screaming changes, becomes something human and mundane. A siren, and then another, wailing into the night. People laying on their horns like it's the solution to their problems.

My next breath in is shivery and calming. The sheen of pungent, terrified sweat cools on my skin. The earthy decay of river water is gone, and sweet air fills me in a steady, freeing rhythm.

I'm okay.

The siren wails again, and I sink back into my pillow, trying to bury the sound, but the tin-thin walls weren't built to keep it out. Or the cold. Or the wet, for that matter, if the budding mold in my kitchen is any indication.

There's a thud outside my door, a hurried clatter of boots. More arguments and shouting. It's the usual mess of my neighbors, but it's late, even for them. I rub my hand over my gritty eyes.

For a sleepy moment, I almost call out to Gran to find out what's happening—she's terribly nosy, so she's likely already at the window with the curtains cracked, making notes for Sunday's after-church brunch gossip—but when I drowsily sit up, I'm not in our trailer.

Shadows claw their way toward my bed.

My pulse starts to race again, and a book slips off my pillow, snapping shut with a clarifying *clap*. I blink down at it.

The savaged head of a bloody pig stares accusingly back at me.

I flinch.

My heart patters uncomfortably as I stare at the illustration, remembering conches and fires and woodland glades. Words.

They're just words on a page. Sure, they might inspire change—or nightmares—but they can't hurt me. Not now. Not directly.

But deep, primal dread still clings to me, cobwebbing my usual rationality. It's too late to be awake. The room's shadows warp and every sound is a threat.

Nothing feels safe when you're alone in the dark.

It's a long, slow moment before I pick up the book. The second-hand copy of *Lord of the Flies* is tattered and worn, its cover a grisly homage to my dream.

Uneasiness unfurling in my stomach, I slap it face-down on the bed.

Eden, you're being ridiculous.

It's just a room, and it's just a book.

Something slams against my door, and I scream.

That was not just a book.

No. No, no, no. Not tonight.

Fumbling at my side table, I grab my glasses and shove them on. The awful, stretching shadows become edged, real, and slowly, my grip on my bedsheets eases.

There's nothing deadly here, right? It's just the same worn, empty studio I fell asleep in. It's safe. It's fine. All predictably ordinary.

I pull my covers up to my chin.

My ordinary lawyer's bills are still strewn across the table. My ordinary divorce certificate is out, so I could fill out my ordinary name change application. My ordinary work schedule hangs on my fridge, with only half the ordinary shifts I need to work to make rent. The ordinary photo of my gran sits by my bedside, her favorite cross necklace hanging from its frame. And there's no point in calling out to her to ask her for gossip, because she died two years ago, in a very ordinary way.

There's nothing preternatural coming to get me.

Another thud echoes in the hall, then a clatter in the stairwell . . . and my stomach flips squeamishly.

Not ordinary. That was *not* ordinary.

I throw my covers back, and edge out of bed, staring at my door.

"Hello?" I call out—and immediately wince at the tremor in my voice.

Brilliant. Wonderful. Why not just announce *that you're prey next time?*

"*Come on in, Mr. Murderer, sir. Oh no, I'm entirely alone—and entirely lacking a social life. It'll be days before anyone thinks to look for my cold, dismembered* corpse.*"*

But no one answers my tentative question.

I shift my weight from foot to foot, unsure what to do. I wonder, briefly, whether I should call the police, but dismiss the idea almost as soon as it comes. I've called them far too many times from my old trailer—after listening to my neighbors' fights take on the kind of drunken ferocity that chills me to my bone—only for no one to show up. Maybe it would be different here, now that I'm no longer living in that trailer park . . . but I still don't think my neighborhood is wealthy enough for quick justice.

Car horns blare from the street outside, and I jump at those too, the realization that something is *happening* finally catching up with my sleepy brain. It shouldn't be this loud. Not at this time of night. Not here.

My door bangs again, and I bend down to pick up the baseball bat tucked under my bed. My trembling hands sweat around the rubber grip, but I cling to it for dear life as I creep toward the door.

Is it a raid? Someone cooking up something they shouldn't? Or maybe there's an event on, somewhere, that I didn't know about. At night. On the edge of town.

No, don't be stupid, Eden. That's ridiculous.

It's definitely a demon.

Oh no, I never had the depth perception for baseball. I know how to use this bat about as well as I know how to load a bazooka.

Holding my breath, I peer through my peephole, half-sure I'm going to see an eye staring back.

I don't, but what I do see is just as concerning.

I open my door, frowning. "Mr. Flores? Is everything okay?"

He spins on the too-dark stairs, his eyes wide, and his enormous suitcase smacks against the railing. "Mrs. Hargreaves? What are you still doing here?"

"Oh, well, it's Ms. Anderson now. Can I ask, what are you—"

"You need to leave. Now!" Sweaty, panting heavily, my next-door neighbor stares at me, seemingly panicked. "You haven't heard the broadcast?"

My uneasiness returns with a vengeance. "What broadcast?"

"What—?!" The sharp, abrupt pitch of his voice makes me flinch, and he stops, shaking his head like he doesn't know where to start. He swallows. "We've been attacked. Nuclear. Cities, Eden. So many cities. I . . ."

"Julian?" a woman shouts from downstairs, her voice anxious, and Mr. Flores looks down the stairwell urgently.

My stomach crawls into my throat, lumpy and full of bile. My thoughts are sluggish and unhelpful. "I'm sorry, what do you . . .?" I stare at him. Confused, I lift my hand to my messy sleep-mussed hair—until I remember I'm still holding the bat. I lower it. "*Which* cities? By *who*? Why would they . . ."

"Julian, we need to *go*! They're putting up roadblocks."

I stare at the shadowy stairwell, my breathing starting to come in panicky hitches. It's Nadine. Mrs. Flores. She leaves empanadas on my front doorstep in exchange for cookies. She's usually so soft spoken, but that . . .

The bat falls from my numb hands.

Mr. Flores shakes his dark, curly head, edging backward. "Not Harlow. Not yet. I'm sorry, I can't—"

"Julian!"

He sighs, rough and rattled. My gaze swings wildly between him and the stairwell. The noises outside are growing, crashing together in a sea of desolate fear and angry desperation.

"You should go. Be with your people, your family. Just find a radio. Listen to the cities, I—"

"But I . . . I . . . don't have any people," I stammer, bewildered.

"Julian, *now*!"

Mr. Flores swallows, then looks at me pleadingly. "I'm sorry. I'm sorry." He backs down the stairs, dragging his suitcase. It smacks on every step.

He's *sorry*?

Fear clutches my gut, and I rush toward the staircase, bending over it to plead down at him. "No, wait. Please. Please wait. Don't leave me. Please, just wait."

But he doesn't stop moving. Every crashing step stokes my alarm. My thoughts are coming in dizzying, panicky swirls.

Attack. Nuclear.

I grip the railing, and my terror rips free. "What am I meant to *do*?"

My shout echoes through the empty halls.

He finally stops in the stairwell, half lost to the shadows, and his face crumples.

When he finally looks up at me, there's a wet shine to his dark, guilty eyes that chills me to my marrow.

"I can't help you, I'm sorry."

He disappears into the darkness.

And leaves me alone.

I STAGGER BACK into my apartment, stumbling over the bat. I grab it as I step inside and slam my door shut against the lightless hall.

Attack. Nuclear.

He's not . . .

That can't be . . .

Another car screams outside my window and it's too *dark*. I flick on my apartment light, but the bulb doesn't obey. I flip it up and down again with more urgency, but there's not so much as a flicker, and I slam my shaking hand against it.

No.

Storming to the window, I fling open the curtains.

Up and down the street, as far as I can see, taillights glow in infernal orange and red, headlights glare in medicinal white. Cars kiss each other, bumper to bumper, flooding both lanes of traffic, moving in a glacial crawl.

My unwilling gaze tracks the long, stretching lines of cars.

On, and on, and on.

They're fleeing town.

I bend over, trying to breathe as the sounds of car horns swamp me. People shouting. Doors slamming.

Attack. Nuclear.

Dread swamps me. Rushes into my nose and chokes my throat like nightmares and river water. Get a radio, he said, but I don't *have* a radio. This can't be real. It's something else, something . . . something *ordinary*.

Rushing to my bedside, I clutch at my phone. I don't have anyone to call—I have exactly three contacts on my phone, and I doubt my lawyer, my manager at the library, or my old college study group organizer will answer me right now—but if I can just *search*, get some information, then maybe . . .

There's a single unread message on my phone.

It takes my clammy, quaking thumb two tries to open it.

> This is a message from the Federal Emergency Management Agency: nuclear detonations have occurred in multiple locations across the country. To protect yourself and your family, get inside, stay inside, and stay tuned for more information. Move to the lowest level and most interior portion of the building if possible. Follow instructions from officials—this can save your life. Martial law is now in place.

I freeze.

I read it again. The message doesn't change, but I try twice more for good measure. I half shake my head, like the silent denial will change the words on my screen.

No. No, this is a bad joke. AI nonsense, or some scam or troll or . . . or *something*.

My stomach turns jittery, fizzling. This isn't right.

Pulling up social media, I search *nuclear strike USA*, but my feed doesn't populate, and it only takes me a single, sick-stomached moment to realize I don't have a signal.

I have no Wi-Fi at all. No power. No cell service. No news.

My vision blurs. What . . . do I do? Even if I leave town, I don't have anywhere to *go*. No long-lost aunts with summer homes or ride-or-die besties who would take me in.

My hollow, empty studio mocks me. My divorce papers. Mrs. Flores's empanadas.

The dried, lonely tears still clinging to my pillow.

I . . . I don't have *anyone*.

They all left me alone.

Oh God, how do I . . .? What am I meant to . . .?

There's a sharp, rapid burst of gunfire outside my window, and I jump back from it, trying not to hyperventilate.

Panic has me by the throat as I snatch up a backpack and start stuffing it with clothes. Essentials only. Warm clothes. Clothes I can move in.

My terror is clouding my thoughts, but I *need* to think. *Nuclear* and *attack* are too big for me to handle right now, so I try something smaller. The immediate problem. The immediate solutions.

What do I need? Where did I last see it? Will it fit in my bag?

Supplies join the clothes in the backpack. Cans. Pouches. Bars. Foods that last. Nothing *too* heavy. A lighter. Water bottle. First aid kit. Flashlight. My empty apartment taunts me with its miserable lack of guns and toilet paper.

I don't have anywhere *near* enough toilet paper for an apocalypse.

I shove a few rolls in anyway.

Every immediate solution is another breath. Another salve

against my raw, throbbing panic. But one question storms past all my attempts at calm.

Where do I go? Where do I go? Where do I go?

There's another burst of gunshots outside, and I jump, my glasses slipping down. A sob escapes me, but I rip off my pajamas and get dressed. I pointedly ignore how worn through the soles are on my threadbare boots as I shove them on. They're the most comfortable shoes I own, and I have no choice.

Where do I go?

I leap to my feet. Right now, it doesn't matter where I go, as long as it's not here.

I just need to find the next safe place.

Glass shatters, too close, and I pause, wavering as I haul my heavy backpack over my shoulders.

Was that the store downstairs?

Dread creeps in alongside my panic. I've seen looting before, and this hot, nervy restlessness is too familiar. I need to get out before it gets out of control.

I scan my tiny, cramped studio for anything I've missed in my packing, and it hits me that this could be the last time I see it. It's not much, but it was never as bad as Henry made it out to be. It was safe enough. Comfortable. Not too far from the library. As far as places go, I've certainly lived in worse.

It could have been a home, if he'd let it be.

My chest aches.

I haven't packed sentimentally. I don't have many items I feel sentimental *about*, but I still find my gaze pausing on my grandmother's photo.

She stands beside me at my high school graduation in a military-tight bun and her Sunday best, her gaze slightly off center.

Her necklace—a dark red stone cross—sits neatly around her neck.

The same necklace dangles from the photo frame.

Another gun fires outside, and I kick myself for delaying. The frame itself is too big to be practical, but . . .

On instinct, I pick up the necklace, and the chain links slide between my fingers as I slip it over my head, then tuck it under my shirt.

I'm not really sure why I do it. The stone is chipped. Cheap. Hardly imbued with the power of Christ or protective strength, as my grandmother believed.

But right now, when being alone suddenly feels terrifying . . . I want it with me.

A reminder of the only family I ever had, pressed close against my chest.

Cold, numb with fear, I pick up the baseball bat.

And, with gunfire and carnage raging behind me, I leave my past behind.

I FLY DOWN concrete steps and burst out onto the pavement.

And into anarchy.

People are pouring out of cars and onto the road. Parents are running with their children in their arms, away from the gunfire, small bags in tow. There's a young blonde woman ducked down beside her car door, frantically repacking the contents of her suitcase into a backpack. A skinny man is standing in his trailer among cases of bottled water and heavy gas canisters, pointing his gun at a small pack of encroaching men. An American flag billows from the back of a truck behind him.

The auto parts store is busted open, and Arnie's newly stenciled window lies in a thousand shards on the sidewalk. I back away from it, my throat raw at the sight.

It shouldn't matter. Not now.

But he was so proud of that window.

"*You* fucking move! I'm blocked in—go left!" someone yells, and I pivot to keep them in sight, only for another stream of curses to burst behind me. A shot.

The sounds are too loud, and they come from all sides. Horns and shots and shouting.

A murky, lumbering figure climbs out of Arnie's store, a car battery under one arm and oil under the other. There's no overhead halo of streetlights, so I can't make out his features as he turns to me.

Only his eyes gleam in the dark.

Not safe, not safe, not safe.

Scrambling, I take off down a side street. My backpack strains my shoulders and slams against my lower back as I run, but I don't care. I turn through alleys and streets, darting away from every shout and gun muzzle and panicked face I can see.

I need to get to . . . to . . .

I stagger out onto another street by the town square, and I bend over, gasping for air for an entirely different reason.

Oh no. Not good. I have *not* done enough cardio to handle an apocalypse.

My glasses drop off my face, and I swipe them back up with a scowl, straightening as I pant.

Cheap backup glasses a size too large are also not ideal. Noted. Wonderful.

Maybe I'll write a book—*How to Survive a Nuclear War: A Librarian's Guide to Not Being a Useless Sack of Potatoes*. At this point, I'm learning by failing. If I survive, I might actually have some good content.

Hidden in the shadows, I rest one hand against the brick and take in the town square.

It's quieter here, and it looks . . . different.

People are moving, moving fast, but this time, they're all heading in one direction, and it isn't out of town. Holding a flashlight that glows like a beacon, a sheriff's deputy is walking the line, beckoning people and pointing them north.

I frown, trying to remember what lies north. The library, of course. The bank. There's a supermarket that takes up two whole blocks and the high school sits behind it. The hospital is northwest—could that be it?

A family passes through the deputy's protective nimbus. An elderly couple. He puts the flashlight down briefly to help a man in a wheelchair down several stairs before he picks it up again.

Watching, I waver, anxiety still squeezing from my pores.

No, stop being hysterical, Eden.

This makes sense. This is what law enforcement is here for. County sheriffs and deputized police, they get manuals on this sort of thing, right? Training? They'll have rules and resources, probably, and information. I can't make good decisions without information now, can I?

I ignore the voice in me that questions whether it matters— the who and the why. Whether more information really will do me any good at all. Whether there really is *any* adequate response to a *nuclear war*, or how local law enforcement could possibly do anything at all to keep us safe from that kind of attack.

It doesn't matter to me who is trying to kill us.

All I care about is who is most likely to keep me alive.

So, it makes sense. I should follow the herd. There is *nothing* wrong with herds. That's how animals keep safe, isn't it? They let many eyes and many ears keep the majority safe?

Only . . . it's not really *my* herd.

A man tugs a woman to a halt. Caught in the deputy's light, he bends down to tie up her shoelaces, and she rolls her eyes with a huffed, emotional laugh that catches me in the chest. When he stands, she melts into his side as they hurry into the night.

I swallow as the shadows press around me.

My lower lip begins to waver as loneliness fills my throat. Looking down, I check my shoelaces and, through a damp blur, and I see they're undone on one side. They're undone, and I'm going to trip and fall and no one is going to help me up. No one is going to watch my back if there's danger. No one cares if I live or die or become fodder for another man's war.

Is it too much, to wish for more?

To want someone . . . *kind*?

Gran's necklace slides against my skin, and I grab hold of it under my shirt. It's cool and steadying as reason through my fear.

It's just adrenaline. You're okay. It will be okay. Just . . . just solve the next problem.

I kneel and tie up my shoelaces with shaking hands.

It makes the perfect bow.

Okay. So I don't have my own herd, so what? I have eyes. Mildly ineffective ones, true, but they work. I'll just . . . I'll just watch out for myself. It might even be easier, not worrying about anyone else.

I can do this. I can be logical.

If the officials are saying we should go this way, then I should take their advice.

My shoulders firming, I stride toward the deputy, falling in among the other people as they move through the gloomy streets. He smiles at me as I pass him, giving me a small nod that shouldn't feel as reassuring as it does.

"To the high school football field, ma'am. We're setting up an evacuation point," he tells me, and his voice is as much of a balm as the light from his flashlight, calm and easy. He flips it casually.

My chest tightens, fills with poisoned, bittersweet hope.

Maybe it *will* be fine.

He's lustrous, his features vague and angelic under his guiding light, and I smile back. Awkwardly, I tuck my bat behind me.

Can I get in trouble for that?

"Thank you, deputy."

They have this.

Something happened, and it was unexpected, and people are naturally reacting out of fear, but they *have* this. They're trained and ready and capable, and I need to stop letting my past dictate my actions, because it's going to get me killed.

I can trust them.

I can trust them to keep me safe.

I can still hear the distant screech of wheels and the patter of gunfire, but it feels far away now, and the trudge toward the high school is eerily familiar. I walk the same way to work most days. Over these steps and into that post office to mail letters.

But it's different in the swampy night, when the clap of footsteps feels thunderous and thick, anxious sweat sours the alley airways.

It's like whispering through a jungle to avoid predators.

Only the trees are buildings, and the prowling predators are strange and unknowable. Faceless creatures with their hands on triggers half a world away.

The deputy's light finally falls out of sight, eclipsed by buildings and bodies, and I wait for another beacon to appear, for the next official to usher us on . . . but no one does.

It's fine, I reason. More than okay. We're only a mid-sized town. Our county is small, but our sheriff's department still has other places to care for. Other towns to divide resources between. It makes sense that there aren't many officers out. There are probably more at the evacuation point, preparing for our arrival. That's all.

I glance up, hoping for starshine and moonlight, but the thick, smoggy clouds roll on, bitterly suffocating the light.

My backpack cuts harsh lines into my shoulders, and my back begins to ache, and I regret packing so much. It was alarmist, and likely unnecessary, I'm sure. Mr. Flores just startled me. Nuclear action is horrifying, but we have one of the largest militaries in the world—if someone bombed one or two of our cities, our government's response will be prodigious.

I'm sure things will be tougher over the next few years, but there are systems in place for this. I'll probably be back home and waiting things out in Harlow for a while.

We pass the bank, then my library, with its charming double doors, and shoulders begin to bump against mine. The crowd edges together against the oppressive dark like we truly are a herd, moving together toward safety.

Up ahead, noises are growing louder, more chaotic again in a way that has me tensing. The people around me start muttering, groaning to their friends and family members in bovine worry.

I stay quiet . . . but cautiously, I bring my bat around again, keeping my eyes scanning the dim streets around us.

We turn a corner, and the supermarket looms large, a swarming crowd of people in front of it. They push and shout and buzz with electric energy. Cars are parked haphazardly in the parking lot, on the street, diagonally over well-manicured gardens, abandoned without care. There are lights, too, but this time, it's not the radiant halo of flashlights. The colors turn over the crowd like a warning and a promise, by turns ominous and hopeful.

Red, blue, red, blue.

Police.

My caution doesn't shift, though several older women around me murmur their relief, and I slow my footsteps. There's something about the people teeming around the supermarket, pressing against its doors that makes me adjust my backpack and stop.

That herd . . . doesn't look like one I want to join.

A new sound—a megaphone, I think—crackles over the low roar.

"It is not safe to leave Harlow. I repeat, it is *not* safe to leave Harlow. Return to your vehicles. Please remain calm. Local enforcement is now working to redirect traffic. In the interest of public safety, roadblocks are being enforced. At the earliest opportunity, please return your vehicles home, then proceed to the evacuation point at the football field for further instructions. Looting will not be tolerated. Anyone who does not follow these instructions may face criminal charges." There's a brief silence, then, "It is not safe to leave Harlow. I repeat, it is *not* safe to leave Harlow. Return to your vehicles. Please remain calm. Local enforcement is now working to . . ."

The blaring voice continues its recitation, and my throat tightens as twin instincts war inside me.

I understand the need to follow a rule of law. I *like* rules, generally speaking. They make order from chaos. Provide stability, *predictability*, when everything becomes unpredictable. I even understand that it's unsafe for people to be fleeing, congesting the roads and barreling headfirst into potentially deadly situations. And the deputy was kind. He was helping, and calm.

He *had* this.

So maybe it's fine. I'm overreacting again.

I mean, no, talk of *criminal charges* and *roadblocks* isn't exactly calming my agitated nerves. And yes, the feeling of being penned in makes me want to bolt free of my cage, but that's *natural* for livestock. Which is what I want to be. Safe. In a group. It's far better than trying to go this alone, with no information or skills or place to go.

Truly, they should call it *alive*-stock.

Really, the police are just like . . . shepherds . . . herding the flock. Ranchers, directing the herd.

My stomach churning, I let the crowd pass me.

So why can't I shake the image of wolves biting at our ankles?

Apparently, I'm not the only one.

"Fuck you, and fuck your criminal charges!" a man shouts.

"Where the fuck do you get off?"

I'm jostled hard by a man from behind, and my glasses fall off again.

"This is America!"

Frantically, I bend, only just snatching them up before a heavy boot crunches down on top of them.

The megaphone grows louder, the lights become blinding. *Red, blue, red, blue.* "Return to your vehicles. Remain calm. Looting will not be tolerated . . ."

A supermarket window breaks, followed by a triumphant, chaotic roar, and someone knocks me from my crouch onto my hands and knees as they stampede forward.

On second thought, livestock usually gets slaughtered.

Or—at this rate—trampled.

I'm tossed, shoved, and it takes everything to haul myself to my feet and break free of the crowd. I flatten myself against a wall, lifting my shirt with a whimper. Bruises are already flowering in aching jabs over my soft stomach and my left thigh is numb where someone kneed me. I flex my fingers—half-crushed but still functioning.

"*Return* to your *vehicle*," the officer outside snaps into the megaphone. Now that he's not reading the script, I realize how *young* he sounds. "No—no looting!"

Another window shatters, this time closer—a different store —and I kick myself for stopping even for a moment.

Run. Move.

My thighs burn as I push against the crowd, trying to go back the way I came. The evacuation point might be past the supermarket, but the supermarket is a powder keg starting to burn, and I *refuse* to be there when it goes off.

A large man slaps me, and I stagger back against another wall, clutching my face. Shocked, painful tears spring to my eyes at the sudden, livid pain bursting along my cheekbone. He shoulders through another woman, not even pausing.

"Order! Everybody, remain *calm!*" the voice on the megaphone shouts. "No, *stop—*"

Gunshots explode from the parking lot. A brief, blistering burst that stirs up a wave of shouts and screams. "I told you to keep *order!*"

Shaking, I run my fingers along my tender cheek, confused, frightened tears escaping me.

I didn't do anything.

Why did he hit me?

I didn't do anything.

There's a beat of silence in the megaphone, then a muffled clatter. A squeal.

Then a new voice growls into the megaphone. "Get fucked and die, piggy."

Bang.

The single burst is deafening. Vile.

My hand stops massaging my cheek, and I feel the thud of the slumping, weighted fall in my chest.

Did they . . .?

Surely they didn't just . . .?

There's a hollering, raging roar in response, and all I can picture is the gruesome pig's head on my book cover, bleeding onto my bed. Young boys dancing around a pagan fire.

They killed him. They killed Piggy.

The screams around me turn vague and waspish. The clouds part enough to give a silvered, otherworldly glow to the buildings and winding streets. To the terrified faces of people running past me, screaming.

They killed him.

They're *killing*.

I back away from the supermarket, away from the crowd swarming into the supermarket and engulfing the police car like a wave. I take off back into town, away from the madness and the killing, rounding corners with skidding, desperate speed.

Buildings flash past me like towering trees. Hot air whips my cheeks. It *is* a jungle. That's what they call it, isn't it? An urban jungle?

I was wrong. The predators aren't half a world away. They're friends and neighbors, and they weren't a herd at all.

They're a pack.

I jump up a flight of stairs, sobbing when my weak legs quiver, threatening to give out when I reach the top step. A bearded man runs past me, clutching a bag, and someone tackles him from behind. They tumble down the concrete steps with crashing, bone-cracking violence.

Oh God, oh God.

A sick moan escapes me as I force myself to move.

It's a hunt. A killing. But there's nothing *urbane* about it. There's not even a semblance of ritual or . . . or *meaning*. It's just fear and self-preservation. Just predator and prey, resources and need. The core of survival. Rule number one.

Kill or be killed.

I sob as I dart past another limp body, its neck awkwardly angled over a welcome mat. Rummaging, gnashing sounds crawl from the black depths of the store.

They killed Piggy.

No—I'm Piggy, with my glasses and my fumbling, soft body.

I'm next. Of course I'm next.

I shove sideways to avoid a father dragging his clinging

child. My glasses almost fall again, and I snatch them off my face, holding them as I run. Someone shoots out a window beside me, and I stagger back, changing direction.

It's all a blur. Murky and unedged and nightmarish again, but I can't lose my glasses.

Suddenly, I recognize the street. The hazy poster for the local production of *The Hunchback of Notre Dame*.

The charming, familiar double doors.

When I see the library, tears burst out of me in violent, urgent relief.

Blinded, blurred, seeing the familiar filigree is almost enough to make me fall to my knees. It's my library. My home. My safety and sanctuary.

It's still and silent and untouched, despite the nauseating chaos roaring up and down the street, and I limp toward it, biting back hiccupping sobs that won't stop racking me.

Two men slam their shoulders against door of the convenience store across the road, but they pay me no mind, so I fumble for my keys.

"Hey! Hey, that's my store!" Mr. Johanson appears from behind a building, his shirt torn, and eyes fiery hot. He has a shotgun.

One of the men throws his hands up, falling away from the door, but the other doesn't stop. Quickly, I try to find the key on the chain, but it's dark and they're all so similar. They slip between my violently shaking fingers, and I curse under my breath, sniffing back a cry.

There's a tussle, a loud shot behind me, and I squeeze my eyes closed as I press my forehead against the double doors, locking my mouth tight against a wailing cry.

It doesn't matter.

A woman screams to my left. Screams and screams and screams.

I force my teary eyes open, looking at her as she stares at whatever lies behind me. Screams at it. Screams like she's being rearranged at her core.

She's waifish and young.

She has glasses too.

"Come here," I call softly, my voice hitching. The words are out before I know what I'm saying. It's so hard to force my voice above a whisper. "Here, with me. It's safe. I can . . . I can get in, I just . . ."

The keys slip between my fingers, and I catch them an instant before they fall.

I look up, but I can only see her back as she disappears toward the supermarket.

Damn it. Damn it, damn it, damn it.

I sob again.

And suddenly, a heavy shoulder falls against the door in front of me.

I recoil, a strangled shriek stunned from my throat before I . . . I squint. Hurriedly, I shove my glasses back on, my heart rolling around my chest in strange, shocky ways.

There's no holy nimbus surrounding him now. No bright flashlight sweetening his slightly awkward features and amused eyes.

But I recognize him.

"Deputy?" I whisper.

He shrugs like it's nothing. Like we're out for a coffee date and he's being gently self-deprecating.

"Wednesday through Sunday, and every incoming apocalypse." He nods at the doors, rubbing something white and fluffy between his fingers. "I hear you say you can get in?"

Up the street, a pack of people are hollering and shooting out windows, one by one.

"Probably a good idea to hop to, if you can," he adds.

My pulse throbs at my wrists, my throat, with nerves and relief and urgency and so many other feelings I can't put my finger on.

He looks *normal*. Not crazed and mindless with fear. He's not *hunting*.

He's looking at me, not through me, and that one fact alone makes me feel less like a fading ghost and more like a person again. More like *me*.

"Right," I breathe. "Right, of course."

I step up to the door, my fingers only slightly steadier as I find the next key, then shove it in the hole.

It jams, and I squint.

No, not that one.

I glance at the deputy, but he's watching the street. If he's impatient, he doesn't show it—just keeps watching the pack of men stalking closer through the street.

Swallowing, I fumble for another key, and urgency licks at my skin.

It doesn't even get past the first bite.

"Damn it." I gasp.

I feel him look down at me as I take up the next one.

"So, you brought your work keys for Armageddon?" he asks casually. "I really hope you're getting hazard pay for this."

A pained, pealing cry lights up the night, but he doesn't budge. Just tucks away whatever was in his hands.

Wildly, I look around, then try to shove the key in. I miss the hole. Try again and miss that time too.

Come on, Eden.

"I—" I frown, trying to focus on the question as the cry cuts off with ominous sharpness. "They're just m-my keys. I had to lock up my apartment."

Is he mocking me?

Mocking me *now*?

He unhitches his gun from his holster as someone darts too close, and holds it cautiously against his thigh.

I glance at the hardness of it, the rough sprawl of his hand, then discard another key as my stomach trips. He's warm next to me. Steady. He might not be flashing a guiding, angelic light around, but I feel it anyway—the soft welling of relief as I let him take over.

I keep my eyes on my task. I can afford to, now.

He's watching my back.

My own, two-person herd.

My hands are steadier with the next key I try.

His careful surveillance is at odds with his easy, drawling voice. "No, no, it's very responsible of you. The keys are cute. Hey, can you clear my late fees while we're in there? I want a clean slate for the end of the world."

Okay, maybe he's not that reassuring.

"*Is this* the end of the world?" I ask shrilly.

Not that key either.

I drop it fast, moving on to the next.

He shrugs. "Well, look, I ain't any kind of expert—but when over fifteen major locations get blown into pixie dust, it sure feels like it to me."

I pause and stare up at him, my lips parting.

Fifteen.

Not one or two. Not that one or two is good. It isn't. But *fifteen*. Fifteen is . . .

I close my eyes for a brief, throat-closing moment. *Eden, you fool*.

This is too big to be fixed. Not in a few years.

Maybe not ever.

Someone shoots across our street, and the deputy stiffens, snapping the safety off his gun to shoot back in three punching shots that make my ears ring.

We're done.

"Oh God. This *is* the end of it, isn't it?" The next key I stab in feels like it might work for a useless second before it doesn't. Why do I have so many *keys*! "No. No, it *can't* be. I'm not ready. I've never taken a shot. I never saw Europe. I haven't skinny-dipped on a summer night, or . . . or had a fling with an acrobat."

"Nah, you don't want to skinny-dip. Not on a summer night anyway. Too many mosquitos," he reassures me, but I'm hardly listening.

Only two keys left.

"I haven't had anywhere near enough sex," I hiss.

He snorts, then laughs, pulling up his gun and rolling his back against the doors to look down at me. I feel his eyes twinkling over my face, replacing the stars that should be in the sky.

"Well, now doesn't feel like the most appropriate time to rectify that, but—"

"Oh, shut it," I growl.

Then instantly blush, mortified at my horrific manners, but he only grins at me. Nodding at my keys, he indicates for me to keep moving.

"You know, usually if you beckon someone to safety, you should already have a safe place to beckon them to," he confides, and I narrow my eyes.

I pick up the next key, refocusing on the door. "*Usually*, if a deputy tells you to go on to *safety*, they don't send you into a *war zone*."

The key slides into the lock with a soft *snick*.

But his attention is locked on my face, his lips quirked in amusement. "It's my first week on the job."

"Hey, is someone there?" a drunk, belligerent voice calls, and the deputy looks up.

"Is that a convenience store?"

"Safer than the supermarket."

The deputy's mouth firms, but he knocks up a patient brow for me. "Do you want me to just break a window? I can just break a window if you need help."

I lift my chin. "Don't. You. Dare."

A gun fires right as I turn the key, and the library doors burst open.

WE FALL INSIDE, and the deputy secures the heavy double doors behind us, locking us in darkness.

Inside, it's cool and calm, and the sounds of the chaotic world and blistering gunshots are muted by the library's thick walls. The musty, comforting bookish scents wash over me. Parchment and glue, old and new, they embrace me like relieved friends.

A light flickers, then holds, and I turn to see the deputy rest the flashlight atop the curved information desk. It's not much, but the flaring, silver glow is more than we had outside.

I drop my heavy bag off my shoulders with a soft *oof*, then eye the doors. They're re-locked and thick. Not easy to break into. Not that I can think of many people who'd care to break into a library.

I worry my bottom lip between my teeth. "Do you think Mr. Johanson is okay?"

His brows lift. "Mr. Johanson?"

"He owns the convenience store," I whisper, my arms wrapping around my middle.

He's a grumpy man, but he always said good morning when he saw me. Sometimes it felt like I was invisible from waking to work, until he muttered that greeting.

The deputy gives me a curious look, then peers out the window. His face pales. "Hmm. Balding? Neck rolls and a torn red . . . Oh. Actually, I don't think the shirt is red. Hey, is he skinny with tattoos? Or tall? Goatee? Goatee has a good jump on him, I—"

"Balding," I confirm, trepidatious.

What does he mean, *red shirt*?

"Oh." He winces. "Yeah, he's definitely . . ." He catches my expression and coughs. "Fine. He's *great*."

My hand flutters to my throat, my mouth dropping open as I try to work up a response. My horror, all the nervous dread of the last few hours bubbles up in something like hysteria.

"*Oh*," I huff a wild laugh. "Oh, that's just . . . That is *just* . . ."

I choke, then hold up one finger and turn around, wondering if I'm going to throw up.

My muscles—such as they are—are wobbling under me,

and I lean against the desk. It's not like I'm not active in my job. Mildly, at least. I'm on my feet fairly often. But there's 'library active,' and then there's 'fleeing for your life active.'

And I know bad guys don't typically offer warning when they're, you know, nuking cities and all, but I *really* would have appreciated just a few weeks to at least start *practicing* my marathon running. It seems like part of the survival starter pack, doesn't it? Knowing how to run? If you can't run, you're as good as . . .

I stop.

Mr. Johanson is dead.

He didn't even have time to run.

The thought stops my internal complaints, and my eyes drift shut.

That young policeman is dead.

The body on the welcome mat, its limbs all in a sprawl.

"Are you okay?"

Behind my eyelids, I can only see that body.

"I . . . I never knew that necks could bend at that angle," I tell him in a hush.

My gorge rises, and I only just fall to my knees and toss my glasses aside in time to vomit noisily on the floor. Then again. It drags up my throat and out my mouth hot, violent rushes. It's foul. Sour and wet, and the taste of it clogs my nose and tears stain my face as I retch and retch, and soon I don't know when the vomiting stops and my crying starts.

Something knocks against my chest like it's trying to gain entry.

"Oh God. Oh God, oh God," I gasp between hitching cries. "What is happening?"

"You say that a lot, huh?" the deputy remarks, and I startle, turning to stare at him with tearstained eyes. His jaw catches the light as he tilts his head in question. "You religious then?"

His gaze dips, and I start stiffening warily before I glance down.

My grandmother's cross sits between my breasts.

I lift my hand to it and squeeze, dazed and hollow and . . . lost.

I shake my head once. "No. No, not anymore." Sniffing, I add wetly, "It belonged to my grandmother."

He nods, his face soft, and the cool air takes on a private swirl.

In the gentle light, I can see he's around my age—mid-twenties, maybe. He's not exactly handsome, but there's a warm appeal to his expressive face that makes me forget it quickly. Something confiding and honest in his eyes that makes my cheeks heat.

I think it might be the longest anyone has looked at me in years.

Then he glances away, clearing his throat, and regret stings sharp.

"You know you have a little, uh . . ." He swipes at his chin, and I lift my hand.

There are . . . chunks.

Mortified, I squeal, turning my back on him. Clambering to my feet, I rush over to the information desk and pluck several tissues, wiping my face.

"This your water?" he calls, and there is *far* too much amusement tucked into his question for my liking as he tugs my bottle from the side pocket of my backpack.

"It is," I confirm tightly.

He passes it to me over the desk, then fetches my glasses

from the floor beside my . . . *pile*. I swish the water around my mouth with a wince and surreptitiously spit it into a mug. I think it's Susie's, but she never washes it anyway, so it serves her right.

When he wanders back, he leans over the tall desk, but he doesn't hand my glasses back. He plucks up a length of twine from out of the children's craft box we use every Friday and begins tying an end around one metal temple tip.

The quiet begins to calm the roiling heat in my stomach.

"It's protective, you know," he tells me as the twine loops and loops around my glasses, but he's looking at my necklace. "Great for grounding. Healing."

I stare at him curiously a moment, then laugh in a soft huff. "Ah, so *you're* the religious one."

A rain of gunshots falls outside, but it's muffled, like the violence has been turned down to low as the library cocoons us inside.

He smiles back at me, lifting a shoulder as he begins to tie the twine to the other temple tip. "Naw, I don't know about all that. Don't tell my mama. It's the stone I mean. It'll give you clarity. Courage when you need it. Good one, that. Lucky thing to have. Especially now."

I arch a brow. "Protection. Grounding. Healing. Clarity. Courage. All that from just one stone. Remarkable."

He snorts at my tone.

"Hey, watch it now. You should show some respect." Setting my glasses down, he tugs something out of his pocket and waggles it at me. "I know all about lucky. Certified expert one might even say."

Standing, I stare, horrified, at the . . . the *thing* in his wide hand. I come around to his side of the desk to get a better look at the grotesquerie on his keychain.

"Good grief, is that—"

"My lucky rabbit's foot!" he confirms, his smile tugging up into a lopsided grin.

"Is it . . . *real*?" I ask delicately, staring at the adorable, fluffy tuft.

I know the charms exist. They go back a long time.

I just haven't seen one in person before.

His eyes widen in mock offense, and this close I can see they're a dark, syrupy brown.

"Of course it's real! It's my bunny Lola's foot. She was the most loyal bunny friend a man could have up until she decided to try hitching a ride on a passing tractor. Got herself good and squished, but her foot was all right. I knew a guy and he took good care of her." He takes in my dismayed expression with a smirk, leaning back against the desk in a way that draws his uniformed shirt tight over his chest. "It's all above board. He got all the blood out and everything. Lucky, see?"

I think I might . . . like uniforms. Like *really* like them. I lift my gaze from his chest, strangely flustered, only to catch the twinkle in his eye.

Hoping he can't see through me, I purse my lips, glancing away.

I can't remember the last time someone flirted with me. If that's what this is. *Is* that what this is? *Flirting*?

It's . . . kind of nice.

Even if it does involve roadkill.

"Well, it doesn't seem like Lola had the best luck," I tell him dryly. "Your charm may be faulty."

He scoffs. "She gets to spend her afterlife having adventures with me. What's not lucky about that?"

"I understand the concept of the charm. It's scientific value I might debate." I throw my hands up. "The part I find *strange* is you carrying around the corpse of a beloved pet!"

"Now that ain't fair. You carry your dead grandmammy's necklace around," he points out, and I whirl, incredulous.

"It's not a dismembered limb!"

"It's a keepsake, I don't know what to tell you."

My next quip, whatever it was, dies in my throat. He's close now, or I'm close to him. I'm not sure who moved into who, but his elbow is propped on the information desk, and I'm in his space. Close enough to admire the angle of his jaw and the curl of hair against his temple.

It's warm here. Nice. Like slipping into a bath after a chilly day.

I've had so many long, chilly days.

He smiles sadly, like he can see it, and it's fragile. Delicate. I don't know what to do with this feeling yet, but I want to protect it. I almost want to beg him not to speak, just so I can sit with it for a few moments more.

Hope is crushed far too easily.

It's too rare, and too elusive, and it would be absurd to lean into it.

Because what are the odds?

What are the odds that after years of being alone, after my father ditched me before I was born or my mother left me to chase a high I hope to God was worth it, after being abandoned time and again by my husband, after friends edging away when my divorce and bills and work started swallowing my time and happiness, after we've been *bombed* and the world has started crumbling around us . . . what are the odds that this could be the start of something *good*.

Can a happy ever after even happen when we're drenched in so *much* sadness?

How is it possible that I'm meeting someone like him now? Someone fun and strong and kind. Someone who will help me, right when I need it the most. It doesn't make sense. I don't have that kind of luck, not on an average day, so maybe he is right.

Maybe our charms do work.

"I'm Simon," he murmurs, and I blink, startled.

Simon. My book and the hunt and my glasses all turn together for a moment before it settles. His name is Simon.

Shaking my head at myself, I smile wryly. How did I get to happy ever after before I even got to first names?

Typical.

This is how I ended up with a husband on my eighteenth birthday.

"I'm Eden. Eden Anderson."

I hold out my hand, and he runs his eyes over my face for a moment before he looks down. Quirking a brow, he takes it, then tugs me a stumbling, fluster-footed step closer.

"Hello Eden Anderson." His gaze softens. "I'm very glad to know you."

Are we . . . going to kiss? I really don't know much about these things but it *feels* like a kissing moment.

His eyes darken, but I hesitate.

It's not that I'm opposed, exactly, to the kissing. I just *really* need to brush my teeth before we do it.

I can still taste leftover carrot.

But he doesn't lean in.

Instead, Simon picks up my glasses from the desk, and the long twine he tied dangles from the back. He hangs my glasses around my neck, until they rest securely beside my necklace.

He fixed a problem.

My problem.

He fixed it for me.

I breathe in shakily, touched.

"There. Now you won't go losing sight of me." His fingers brush my cheek, just briefly, then he steps back. "We should make a plan. You know where the maps are? Local? Detailed as possible. Get them for me?"

We.

It's like his light has swamped me, and I just suppress my giddy smile.

It's not just up to me. There's an *us* now. I don't need to solve all the problems myself—not the immediate ones *or* the big ones.

"Simon says?" I ask archly, and a happy, squirming flutter starts up in my stomach when he rolls his eyes.

I think I could get used to it, following orders.

"They're in the back. Let me get them." But I'm already halfway there, and Simon's right behind me. Crouching down, I pull free drawer after drawer. "Topographic or geologic? Never mind, I'll get both. Why not?"

Susie isn't here to scold me for incautious use of library materials.

I'm already rolling them out over one of the large center tables when it finally occurs to me to frown.

"Why do we need these? There's an evacuation point, isn't there? I figured we'd just wait until things died down outside

—" *Poor choice of words, Eden.* "I mean, that we'd wait until things settled down, then we'd go there."

Simon bends over the maps. "Ah, so, about that. We only have two deputies out in Harlow, me and old man Angus, and he was due to retire about ten years ago."

My giddiness begins to fade.

Fast.

"But the evacuation point, you said—"

He looks up at me, nodding. "Yeah, it's there. Or, it's meant to be. But I don't know that it's going to do much good. Only about ten cops phoned in when Angus put the call out, and . . . well, you saw what it was like. I think . . ." Rubbing the back of his neck, he sighs. "I think we might be better off with a different plan." He looks back down at the maps, pointing at a green patch. "Like here. The forest might be good for a bit. My dad used to take me hunting there. We could camp."

I don't look down at the map.

My throat works as I swallow—as I swallow again, and somehow still find no way to dislodge the abrupt lump in it.

"But . . . the people out there. They're relying on that evacuation point." My gaze drops to his uniform, to the shiny badge on his chest. "They're relying on *you.*"

He can't just leave them.

They're alone in the dark.

Simon's brows come down, and his jaw flexes as his eyes skid away. He scoffs, then runs a hand over his jaw. "Look, I've had this job a week. Jokes aside, end of days wasn't in the job description."

I see the fear, the defensiveness—I've been well-trained to spot those—and I know better than to prick at a man's ego, or think I know better, but all I can think of is the terrified faces of the crowd as they scattered.

It's all I can think of, until . . .

"Get fucked and die, Piggy."

I purse my lips before any accusations fly free. That officer died, doing his duty.

I don't want Simon to die.

Simon is the only person who is helping me right now, and I can't do this alone.

"Maybe . . . maybe we should open the doors. We can help people, together. Get them inside?" I don't know why tears are threatening me again. Why I suddenly feel so confused as I whisper, "Other people need a safe place too."

He straightens, shaking his head, and his voice becomes earnest. "No, Eden, it's not safe. I don't want you in danger."

The thought is briefly warming, but it quickly fades to ash.

He doesn't want *me* in danger . . . or himself?

The thought is unkind, and I berate myself for it immediately. I saw him helping people. The man in the wheelchair. The families. The couple with the shoelaces.

He turned up, when so many didn't.

He's *good*.

Bolstered, I urge delicately, "We can be careful. We can save people. They're dying out there."

Simon studies me. Slowly, he walks back over, until he's in my space again, large and steady and warm. He runs the backs of his fingers over my cheek.

No. The bruise, where that man slapped me for no good reason. It aches, even under the gentle touch.

"There's no saving those people now, Eden Anderson. I want to as much as you do, I swear. But there's nothing we can do. Not when they're like that. You'll only get yourself killed," he whispers.

My breath catches, and I turn my cheek into his touch. It's only partially to hide my face.

He knows better, doesn't he? With all his training?

He knows better than me?

"So we . . . we don't help anyone else?" I wet my dry lips. "We just let them . . . die?"

His hand cups my jaw, and he bends to peer into my face. "No, *no*, I didn't mean that. You can help them. Sure, we can help them. We just . . . don't risk our lives to do it, you know?"

Slippery feelings thread through my warmth. Uncomfortable, guilty pangs.

Silent, I meet his eyes—the syrupy brown, bright with concern and the reflected shine of the light.

Is that the only reason he helped me? The families? The man in the wheelchair? Because it didn't risk his life?

Don't be silly, Eden—of course it is.

Angry heat burns behind my eyes, and I press my lips tight as I scold myself. I scold myself for the hope and the giddiness and for being a stupid little girl who imagines happy ever afters after five minutes of kindness.

I'm a stranger, and people just don't risk their lives for strangers. Bravery like that is for storybooks.

It doesn't exist in the real world.

I don't voice the thought, but shame flashes through his eyes as if he hears it anyway. "Look, you've got to look out for yourself first. You think anyone out there is doing any different? Keep yourself alive. Don't put yourself in danger for anyone else, Eden Anderson, not for anything. They won't do the same for you."

My throat cords as I hold back miserable, hateful tears. They well up anyway.

With every word, he confirms all my worst, most private fears.

I think of Henry. Of Mr. Flores, leaving me alone on the stairwell. And I can't even blame him. Them. Any of them.

Because it makes sense.

Of course you should save yourself. I've thought it before. I felt it, out in that crowd, and I think I've known it most of my life.

I'm the only one watching my back.

I drag in a pained breath. I can't trust my voice just yet so I only nod to him, then turn back to the map.

How many people are hurting right now? How many people are as scared as me?

My tears smudge the ink.

Wet, miserable drops.

"This . . . this forest is better," I finally whisper. "It's farther, but it's deep. We . . . we can hide better there."

I don't even have the presence of mind to couch my suggestion as a question.

God, is this who we are now? Is this what the world *is*? People who don't step out of their bubble to help others? People who are hurt or afraid, who need medicine and care, and who are in desperate need of big, fearless hearts . . . and not this shriveled, *cowardly* thing I have?

I've always thought of myself as good. Less than some, of course, but I'm a *good* person. I am kind to strangers and I donate my change. I'm polite and follow the law and— damn it —none of it *matters*.

I'm not good.

Surely I can't be, the world can't be, if we only help when it costs us *nothing*.

Maybe there is a beast . . . Maybe it's only us.

More tears fall, and I swipe them away.

Good or not, that doesn't matter either. I'm safe, and I'm not alone. That's all that matters, isn't it? When it comes to survival? The next day is all that matters.

So why, even though I'm in this haven with a nice boy and his pretty mouth . . . do I suddenly feel so very much alone again.

In moments, I'm being wrapped up in gentle arms, and he's murmuring apologies into my hair. I stay there, maybe for hours, with my face buried against his chest. I stay there until the muted screams stop outside and the gunfire falls silent.

That's it then, I think. My eyes are raw from crying. *Simon said, and it is so.*

We're safe.

I wonder how many people died on our welcome mat so we could stay that way?

I pull back, letting him move away to trace out the path from Harlow to the forest.

Eventually, Simon rolls up the map, then squeezes my arm. "Come on, we should go while it's quiet."

Numb, I nod, then collect up my bag. We're almost at the door when he pulls me to a stop.

"It's okay, you know?" he says softly. "It's really okay to choose yourself."

From somewhere, I work up a smile for him. It doesn't fit right, but I'm not sure he can tell. His hand drops to mine, gripping it tight.

I look at the join, my heart bruised.

I don't want to live in a world where everyone only chooses themselves.

"Maybe we can choose each other." I glance up, and I almost smile at the surprised pink that stains his cheeks.

Simon searches my face for a long moment, then squeezes my palm. "I'd like that, Eden Anderson."

It stings my throat, but my smile becomes more real, and he winks, then unholsters his gun as I pull my keys back out.

Peering out the window, he nods, so I unlock the doors, and he comes over to crack them open.

Then, hand in hand, we creep out into the night.

Simon steers me through the street, angling his body to block the convenience store. Again and again, he turns me to avoid crimson puddles and fleshy lumps, and I let him.

It doesn't stop the sticky self-loathing from working its way under my skin.

They were *so close*.

So close, and I did nothing.

It's past midnight now, maybe well past, but the moon is hiding from us, and I don't know how to tell the time for sure now that my phone has died. I don't think it matters.

Neither the night, nor Simon, can hide everything.

I still see them as we turn into the next street. A boot here. A ponytail dipping in the gutter there. I can't smell books anymore—only urine and feces.

Simon's hand stays in mine, dragging me forward.

He's right, though.

It's so very, very quiet.

At least, until it isn't.

There's a shift in the shadowed alley ahead, and I immediately pull back on his hand.

"Stop. Simon, stop," I whisper when he tugs me harder.

He frowns, then glances at the shadows. They're now still—and so very quiet.

I eye the alley, darker, blacker than the rest, all my instincts prickling. "Another way."

"*This* is the way." He squeezes my hand and waves the gun in his other. "Trust me, okay? I have this."

He *has* this.

It's what I thought earlier, wasn't it? He's the one with the training. *I* only have feelings—and that doesn't seem like so very much at all.

So why won't they stop *screaming*?

As we get closer, tension winds around me in knotted, anxious loops. Maybe we should just go back to the library. Wait until dawn. It's only two streets away.

But it's too late.

We're almost beside the alley, and I can't breathe for the dread.

It's there.

The shadows shift again, and I scream in terror. A can clatters. Metal glints, and my ears ring like pealing bells, as a garbage bag bursts open, and why is it so *loud*?

I yank my hand back as Simon shoots into the shadows with a curse, but it goes wide.

"Fuck, Eden. What are you doing?"

His curse sounds far away.

He lets my hand go, swearing again as he swings back to the alley, lifting his gun with panic in his eyes . . .

And then he staggers back.

Stops.

He stops, and at first, I don't understand it.

A double-barreled shotgun clatters to the ground, and I stare at it.

Gently, a slender, hollow-cheeked woman steps from the dark, and she takes the gun from Simon's raised hand. It slips free easily. Like a last breath.

"What . . . what did you do?" I whisper, and she startles, clutching the gun to her chest.

I know her.

I stare at her glasses.

I remember her screams and her back as she ran. I tried to save her, and still she . . . she . . .

"I needed it," she pleads. "I was almost out, so I needed it. I need it more than him."

She's just a waif, a teenager, her cheeks silvered with tears.

A shotgun at her feet.

"Why is there blood on your hands?" I ask, confused.

It's splattered her.

Not just her hands. Her cheeks, her chest. She's covered in red rain.

"There isn't." She sobs, backing away.

Simon drops to one knee, touching his stomach. His hand comes away red, too.

"Why is there blood on your hands, Simon?" I ask, but tears are already running down my face, and the words are a moan of denial.

"There's not!" the girl shouts.

She turns, with silver on her cheeks and red on her hands, running away from us with Simon's gun.

Alone.

She's alone, I'm alone.

We're all so, so alone.

"Eden? Eden, help. I can't . . . something's . . ." Simon looks up at me, and his face is strained. Uncertain. A vein throbs at his temple. "Something's wrong."

I fall back, then slide down the alley wall as I see the gaping wound in his stomach. His uniform blown open. The dark, growing stain.

"Please don't." Salt stings my lips as I beg him. "Please don't leave me alone."

Fear bleeds into his eyes.

Something soars overhead, low in the sky, but all I can see is the blood. He's leaking out onto the filthy pavement. Another crimson pool to step over. Another red pool to forget.

He clutches at his stomach.

My ears are ringing. I press my palms against my burning eyes. Against the sight of him dying. My glasses fall, fall for the thousandth time tonight, but they catch on the necklace he made me, and I crumple. My stomach cramps as I scream silently into my legs.

"Staunch . . . Eden, staunch it."

"I *can't*." Snot runs from my nose as I groan.

I can't do it.

I can't do this alone.

The clouds above us part, like they're opening doors to somewhere new. Only they're not pearlescent and bright. These clouds are roiling, tumbling—black and grey and livid with electricity.

No one is taking Simon away on wings of comfort.

This is what we deserve.

"Eden, please . . . please help me."

His plea makes me drop my hands, but only to shake my head at him wordlessly.

There's no point. There's a hole the size of my fist in his stomach.

It's not very silent anymore, out here. It's not still. The packs may have moved on to other streets for now, but I can still hear looting and death.

The hunt is still on.

Fear bites into me. Loneliness swallows me.

"It . . . hurts." Tears start slipping over his paling cheeks.

My lip trembles, and my teeth dig into it. The whole alley smells like death.

Don't put yourself in danger for anyone else, Eden Anderson, not for anything.

"I can't stay here," I plead back, shaking with sobs.

Simon falls into the gutter, tipping his head back as he whimpers, and I cry out.

Crawling over to him, I touch his face, then his chest.

"Help," he pants, shocky and short. "Help me."

Blood is pooling in his stomach, and my hands shake as they hover. "I don't know what to do. I can't— I don't know how."

His sweet brown eyes are desperately afraid, and my insides burn with the need to leave.

I don't want to *see this*.

I don't want to watch him die.

I look down the alley, both ways down the street, but they're empty. There's no last-minute rescue. No one risking themselves for anyone else.

No one is coming to help.

Not knowing what else to do, I peel my cardigan off my

trembling shoulders and press it to his stomach, but his imme-diate, blood-curdling scream makes me fall back.

"Shh." I lift my hands frantically, keeping my voice to a tearful hush. "Shh, please. Don't shout. I can't . . ."

The blood soaks my cardigan in moments.

I stumble to my feet, and tears leak from his eyes. Silently, he shakes his head at me.

"I don't know what to do!" I shout, my hands tangling in my hair, then I flinch again, looking down the empty street.

Waiting for another pack to appear.

I can't do this.

I'm not a doctor—not a nurse or a medic or *anyone* useful. I would give anything right now to be someone like that, to *have* someone like that, but I don't. I only have me. I'm only a librarian. I don't know how to do anything. I'm not skilled, or brave, or smart. I'm only a librarian.

Oh God.

I should leave. I *want* to leave. Simon's warnings and cautions and the too-prolific crimson pools on the pavement all tell me I should.

But I don't . . . and it's for all the wrong, worst, most pathetic reasons. It's not because I'm brave, or *good*.

Self-hatred crawls up my throat.

I'm just not ready to be alone yet.

I drop my backpack into the alley, and I kneel back down beside him, my knees soaking in his blood.

"Please don't leave me," Simon whispers, clutching at my shirt. He sounds so much younger as he begs. As he cries into the filthy alley with too much knowledge in his eyes. "I don't want to die."

"I know." I pull in my wavering bottom lip. "I know. I'm *sorry*."

He starts to shake, and I take his hand, pressing the other one to his pallid cheek.

Something clatters in the alley, but even as my instincts warn me away, I don't look up.

I'm not leaving him alone.

Not now.

"I wish I had read more books," I tell him throatily, looking up at the sky. It's dawning from midnight black into a deep indigo. "I wish I knew more. I wish . . ."

Simon chokes, and tears fall over my cheeks as I tilt his head to the side, stroking his hair. His breathing is so hoarse.

"You made me feel special today. Seen. I hope . . . I hope you know . . . how much that meant," I continue, then cut off on a jerky, indrawn breath.

For a little while, I wasn't so alone.

For a little while, I played pretend.

His stomach is shuddering, his skin clammy, but I try to ignore it. I've never seen someone die before, but I know that's what's happening. He's shutting down, bit by bit.

He isn't a hero or a happy ever after.

He isn't a savior with depthless knowledge.

He's just a boy who went to work today and will never go home.

"Don't stop . . ." he murmurs, and his eyes are terrified on mine. "I'm so scared. Please don't go. I can't do this part . . . Can't do it alone."

I shake my head. "I'm not going. I promise."

His eyes squeeze shut, and he rolls his head against the pavement. "*Why?*"

It's okay, you know? It's really okay to choose yourself.

A sob escapes me before I can snatch it back in, and I squeeze his hand. Hard. Just like he squeezed mine before we left the library.

"I don't want to live in a world where people don't take risks for others," I tell him.

At that, he starts to sob quietly, shame so raw on his face that I have to look away from it.

How many people?

How many people could we have kept safe tonight?

His blood pools warmly between us, and his skin grows cooler in my hand.

"Eden . . . Eden . . ."

He begins to repeat my name, over and over, his pretty brown eyes unfocusing, and I trace my thumb over his cheek, whispering nonsense to him. Sweet, soft things. Compliments and comforts that mean less than nothing now.

When he starts growing more agitated, groaning in pain, his body jerking in harsh, uncontrolled movements, I sit up over him.

Tears running down my face, I take my necklace from around my neck. The heavy cross falls into my hands and I press it against his chest.

His eyes lock on my face, bulging and bleak.

"I still don't think it does anything. I don't believe in lucky charms. I don't think stones can be clarifying or grounding, or any of what you said." He cries out, agonized and low, and I swallow before I continue. "I don't believe in it. And that's the first rule of magic, right?" I sob. "You have to believe in it?"

His hands wrap around mine as his body jolts and shudders.

It's not pretty, or peaceful, or any of the things I wanted for him. I'm not sure he can even hear me right now.

But I stay anyway.

"I don't believe in magic, Simon, but you do. And maybe I'm wrong. So, you take it. Take it just in case. Maybe jasper and Lola's dismembered foot will heal you after all, and we can still go to the woods together like we thought?" I bite my lip, then add, "Neither one of us has to be alone, okay? I'm here."

His breathing takes on a darker, hoarser tone, and his jerking begins to slow.

Over and over, I stroke his face. "It's okay. I'm here. I'm not leaving you."

Until finally, his breathing stops.

I STARE at his face for a long, teary moment, waiting for the next inhale that never comes.

I choke on a cry, slumping back. My shoulders shake as the tension drains out of me, and all the sadness and the uselessness of it all seeps in.

He was just a boy.

He didn't know anything—he didn't know what to do, or where to go, and his instincts weren't better than mine. He did his best . . . but he was just a boy. A sweet boy who I trusted more than I should have.

More than myself.

I look down at Simon, at his dead, limp body and the hand that's still wrapped around mine. I pry mine away and, with a sad sniff, I close his palm over my gran's jasper cross, and move it over his chest.

I slide his empty eyes shut.

The sky is dawning now, breaking through patches of thick cloud, and I stand. I pick up my backpack and put it on. I loot Simon's pockets for an extra lighter. I take his water and the maps of the forest, and whatever else looks useful and small enough to carry.

I leave Lola's foot.

I'm not so sure that's the kind of luck I need on my side.

Besides, this way, maybe they can continue their adventures in their afterlife.

With a deep pang in my chest, I lift my glasses from around my neck and slide them back on.

And I walk back to the library.

A numb, distant part of me urges me to run, but another part, one newer, and stronger, and seasoned over the longest night of my life—that part tells me to go slow. To preserve my energy until I need it. It reminds me that I have days and weeks and months and maybe even years of this kind of fear ahead of me.

I need to be smart. I need to be special, and strong, and to learn new skills.

I can't afford to be useless anymore.

Turning the corner, I step over another body, but I don't look down.

Simon didn't have to die tonight. If he'd listened to me, he wouldn't have.

If I'd trusted myself better, he wouldn't have.

He may have been a boy, and maybe I'm just a girl . . . but I knew better than him. About the maps and the alley, at the very least.

Maybe about all of it.

I make it to the front of the library with no gunshots. No packs hunting me. The early morning sunshine makes a mockery of the carnage in the streets. The unhinged doors and shattered glass by several stores, the blood and the bodies collapsed in undignified, final poses.

No one moves.

It's a quiet, peaceful morning.

This time, when I pull out my keys, I get the right one on the first try, and I step inside. It's still dim without the flashlight, but I know this place better than I know my own home. I pass through the aisles, by the wooden shelves and precious books that have been my whole world.

I'm not a doctor.

I'm not a soldier, or an outdoorsman, *my* dad never took me hunting as a child.

But I pluck books off the shelves. Survival craft. Herbology. Basic first aid. Advanced first aid. A beginner's guide to hunting. There's even one here: *How to Survive a Nuclear Apocalypse.*

They're heavy in my arms, and I stuff them into a tote—the only bags we have here, and possibly the worst option for convenient transportation—before I set my shoulders and once again step foot outside.

These books are my parents.

My friends.

My only helpers.

If it's the end of all things, then at least I'll end it with a good book.

And with that, I make my way to the woods.

IT'S A TWO-DAY JOURNEY, but it takes three more than that since I avoid all major roads and thoroughfares. I won't be caught in another mob. Instead, I hike over fields and trek down back streets until the soles of my flimsy boots wear to slivers. I hide from cars and curl my body behind trees when I see a curious face. I push my soft, unaccustomed body to its limits. Nightmares shock me out of my sleep every night. I wake with tears running down my face and sweat soaking my clothes, but I train myself not to cry out . . . because I don't want to be caught.

It's . . . hard. It's impossible, knowing I don't have a safe place to go.

I just know I have to go somewhere.

Somewhere deep. Somewhere alone. Somewhere far, far away from all the people who will get me killed.

I'm trusting myself now.

I'm listening to my instincts.

In the middle of the day, when the fleeing swarms are at their busiest, I find safe nooks to read my books. Slowly, I learn the difference between wild carrots and water hemlock, and how many types of moss can supplement a diet in the wilderness.

The nights turn bitter and cold, but I scavenge a sleeping bag and tough those out too.

But my newfound scraps of bravery falter when I see *them*.

The drones streaking the sky make me fear like I haven't since that first night. Grey and large and lightning fast, I walk past the cratered aftermaths and the corpse sprays they leave in their wake, and I . . . wish.

I wish things were different.

That there was an army rolling in who would save the day. That if I went to a FEMA shelter, like the one in Landsdowne or maybe Howards, I might find real people who would help. I wish that we had a leader who stood for the right things. Who tried. Someone who would bring our world together, instead of splitting it apart.

I wish that Simon were alive and here with me like he was meant to be.

I wish that someone were here, someone I could trust—truly *trust*—to never leave me behind.

Someone who would hold my hand if I lay dying.

But I don't let myself wish for too long. I'm learning to better guard against hope.

On the third day, I find a mostly untouched hardware store. Inside, there's a battery-powered radio, and I pick it up with tentative reluctance.

On the third night, I listen to it by the light of the first fire I managed to build for myself.

". . . *Jim Creek Naval Radio Station. VLF Transmitter Cutler. Houston. Atlanta. Los Angeles . . .*"

The names go on and on . . . and this is why it's better not to wish.

I might not have a team, or a herd. I don't have a lover or friends.

But it's better that way.

Lovers leave. Friends die. And I can let the blood on my clothes be a reminder of how fear takes the herd.

How the bad in them will almost always win out.

How they bring out the worst in me as well.

I'm done with all of them. I'm through living my life for people who never truly cared about me to begin with.

On the final day, when I reach the brink of the forest and stop to rest my aching legs, I play the only working local channel I could find . . . and I cry as I listen to the aged, droning voice.

"See that you are not troubled; for all these things must come to pass, but the end is not yet."

Drones slice the sky overhead. Death on swift wings.

Huddled between the roots of a sprawling tree, I watch with a horror that borders on awe.

"For nation will rise against nation, and kingdom against kingdom. And there will be famines, pestilences, and earthquakes in various places."

When the drones leave, the silence swamps me again. I swallow hard as I clutch my radio more tightly.

The end of all things is quieter than I expected.

I think . . . I think it's going to be quiet for a very long time now.

"All these are the beginning of sorrows."

Finally, I turn the radio off and stand, looking back at the dying sun on the horizon.

And with the silence eating at my bones, I stride into the darkness of the woods.

Alone.

Out now

Ensnared

Four years from now, Dom and the Brutes meet one prim and
proper librarian who changes everything for them

And Eden finally gets to discover what it's like to have a family.

Ensnared is available on Kindle Unlimited!